Black Rose

By
Kris Thompson

First published by The Writer's Coffee Shop, 2014

The Writer's Coffee Shop
(Australia)   PO Box 447 Cherrybrook NSW 2126
(USA)   PO Box 2116 Waxahachie TX 75168

Paperback ISBN- 978-1-61213-246-4
E-book ISBN- 978-1-61213-247-1

A CIP catalogue record for this book is available from the US Congress Library.

Front cover image by Thaigher Lillie,
Back cover image by © ozbyshaka / shutterstock.com
Cover design by Thaigher Lillie

www.thewriterscoffeeshop.com/kthompson

Dedication

This story wouldn't even exist if it wasn't for my wonderful friend, Heather H., so I want to dedicate this book to her. Thank you for believing in me and helping me carve this idea out. I would have been lost without you.

Warning

Black Rose contains scenes that some readers may find disturbing. It is intended for mature audiences only.

Prologue

I knew I had to have Nina the moment I laid eyes on her. She was damn near perfect for me in almost every way. Her firm, toned body was hypnotic in the summer heat. The way her golden hair shone in the sunlight, or how her pink tongue slid across her full lips whenever she took a drink of water damn near made me hard every time. Her long smooth legs taunted me as she walked around in her shorts, and my mouth itched to bite down on her full breasts.

She seemed to command attention everywhere she went. I would watch her laugh with her friends as she shopped for mundane things she didn't need, biding my time until I could take her without being noticed. When I did have her in my arms, I swore I was in heaven. I almost took her right then and there on the quad, feeling as though I had waited long enough. Being limited to watching her from afar the last month had been infuriating. I wanted her in her room, in her chain, devoted and obedient to me.

There was just one thing I wasn't prepared for . . . her strong will.

Truth be told, it was one of the reasons I loved her and wanted her. She could keep me on my toes. She would often pretend to be asleep when I came down, and then would jump on top of me when I got near her. Nina could barely throw a punch, so her struggling was comical at best, but she should have known better. She was mine, and I had told her that from day one. I told all my girls that. They were mine, and they were chosen to keep me happy. Their whole world was to revolve around me and me alone. They breathed because I needed them to. They ate because I allowed it.

They slept because I wanted them rested for my needs. And how did Nina repay me for my generosity? How did that stupid bitch show her respect? She tried to escape.

Stupid little whore.

I finished my cigarette as I sat on a fallen moss-covered log, watching Nina's body begin to go into rigor mortis. All around us, the forest was alive. Too alive for such an occasion. The damned conifer trees and blue spruces swayed back and forth, their disgusting scent making me want to light up again. I hated it, always had, but it would serve its purpose.

I snubbed out the butt of my cigarette on the bottom of my boot and stood. Walking over to Nina, I knelt next to her body. I could have buried her, but then how would I enjoy seeing her corpse begin to rot as I took my morning walk? If I closed my eyes, I could still hear the quiver in her voice and feel the warmth of her skin. My hand stretched out to touch her one last time, but I stopped myself. There was no point. Her warmth had been gone for over an hour.

A wave of anger rolled through me as I took in her collapsed skull. I had been kind to her, at least. I had waited until after she was dead before smashing her face in with a rock and removing her hands. I'll enjoy watching them burn later, or maybe I'll hold onto them. She would belong to me, even in death. No one else would see her pretty face again. No one would claim her. My claim would be final.

We could have been great, Nina, but you had to be so bullheaded. Now I need to find a new girl and start all over again.

Chapter 1

Day One

My chest burned with each breath as I hit the last mile of my morning run. The sun had just begun to peek over the eastern horizon, but most of Boulder was still in shadow. Frost covered the windshields of cars and trucks parked on the street, and dead insects dotted the sidewalk—victims of the sudden change in weather, no doubt. I had to feel a little bad for them. Yesterday, I'd been sweating like a racehorse this far into in my run. Today, my cheeks were barely warm and my ears and nose were icy cold— a fact my boyfriend, Richard, would tease me over when I got home. *If* he didn't throw a fit first.

Richard had always joked that I was insane for waking up at five every morning to run. But in the last few weeks he had spoken out openly against the ritual. I understood why, I really did, but I loved running. To me, it was as much a part of my day as brushing my teeth. Even as I passed the phone pole on the corner, the one plastered with a variety of MISSING posters, I was reluctant to give it up.

When I got home, I made coffee before jumping in the shower. Richard's phone was going off for what I estimated would have been the fifth time. I knew he would hit the snooze button at least two more times before finally rolling out of bed, and I would sit in the kitchen and giggle when he would forget to put on his glasses—again—and stub his toe on his way to the shower.

"Please tell me there is more caffeine."

Leaning against the counter, I lifted my cup to my mouth to hide a smile as he walked into the kitchen in only a pair of jeans, his shaggy brown hair sticking out in every direction, and his tan skin still slightly red from his shower.

He pulled his mug from the rack on the counter and poured himself some coffee.

He sighed after he took a sip. "When is this going to be in IV form? We can fly a man to the moon but we can't make a caffeine IV drip bag. That's just wrong."

"You are such a dork," I said, repeating the same thing I said every time he stayed over.

Richard smiled and made his way over to me, his bright, blue eyes much more alert than they had been. He reached forward and took my coffee mug out of my hands and placed both of ours on the counter. I laughed quietly as he picked me up and settled me on the counter, wrapping his arms around me.

"Good morning, Miss Locke."

I hummed against Richard's lips as he pressed them to mine. Wrapping my legs around his waist, I sank my fingers into his hair and grazed my nails against his scalp.

"Good morning, Mr. Haines."

He kissed me again, with a little more enthusiasm. It made me thankful for the nights he stayed over. These morning kisses were fast becoming the best part of my day.

"You need to finish getting dressed," I mumbled as Richard trailed his lips down my neck.

He chuckled darkly. "I'm much more interested in getting undressed right now."

I moaned, half in desire, half in frustration. "We can't. It's Thursday." He ignored me, and nipped at the zipper on my North Face vest. "Stop, Richard. Class. Nine a.m. Driving, remember?"

He let out a soft growl, but stopped. "Okay, okay . . . are you at least going to have time to meet me for lunch before you take your baby to the doctor?"

It was Thursday, which meant Richard and I both had a morning class at the same time. I had an appointment to get my car serviced in between classes.

"I can stop by for a quick bite, but it will only be for a minute or two. It's a fifteen minute drive to and from the dealership, and I can't be late for my three-thirty class again."

Richard wrapped his arms around me and nuzzled his nose into my hair. "Yeah, but it was worth it last time you were late."

I rolled my eyes and pushed on his chest. "You caught me on a good day," I said, referencing the *one* time we had slipped unnoticed into an empty classroom and locked the door. "So don't expect that to happen again anytime soon."

I met my best friend and roommate, Emma Haines, for a quick snack on campus before running off to our next class. I thanked God every day for bringing Emma into my life, and not just because she was the sweetest person I had ever met, but because she was also the reason I met Richard.

"So why did you stay at Adam's last night?" I asked as I munched on my muffin.

"Because we share a wall, and I didn't feel like hearing you and my brother going at it all night."

I couldn't help the laugh that erupted out of me. I did understand how that could be uncomfortable—I wouldn't want to hear my brother having sex either—but she acted as though I hadn't been listening to her and Adam go at it for years, too.

"Well then, I hate to break it to you, but all we did was study, cook dinner, get some laundry done, and watch a movie in my room."

"Wow, that's really . . . boring. You two are like an old married couple. Except married couples say I love you."

"Not this again." I sighed.

"You two are ridiculous."

I rolled my eyes at Emma and ate the last bite of my muffin.

"I'm serious! Adam and I told each other 'I love you' after a month, so how in the hell have you two lasted a year?"

I walked over to a nearby trashcan and threw away my muffin wrapper. I turned and faced Emma, hearing her let out one of her characteristic dramatic sighs.

"Some things just don't need to be said, Emma. Some things you just already know."

"I get that, I swear I do, but don't you think it may be something my brother would like to hear?"

"Emma, we care about each other, and I know he loves me. I can feel it every time he kisses me, touches me, and . . . screws my brains out."

"Ew! I do not need to hear that!"

I laughed and grabbed her hands away from her ears and raised my voice.

"And if I didn't believe beyond a shadow of a doubt that he felt it, too, I would say something."

"Whatever. I just think things would be beautiful if you two would just say the damn words. You could make it all romantic, like a Nicholas Sparks novel, or something."

Rolling my eyes at her again, I hitched my arm through hers and nodded. "Duly noted."

—⁓—

"So are you going to come over tonight?" I asked, leaning into Richard's side as we left CU on the Run.

"Where else would I want to be?" he said, kissing my hair and wrapping his arm around me.

I stopped right at the edge of the parking lot, taking my backpack from his shoulder and stretching up on my toes to kiss him. "See you in a few hours, then."

I almost laughed as I watched him scan the path to the parking lot over my head, and then check his watch.

"I have time to walk you to your car." Richard took a step forward, but I stopped him.

"No, you don't. I promise to call or text you if I'm running late." I slung my bag over my shoulder and gave his hand a soft squeeze before I started walking toward my car.

"Lee," Richard yelled, and I turned to see a look of worry on his face. "Just please be careful."

I laughed and raised my arms. "I parked next to one of those emergency buttons, remember? Now hurry to class!" I blew him a kiss and turned around, continuing on to my car.

When I reached it, I noticed a white flyer underneath my windshield wiper. I opened my driver door and tossed my bag inside, leaned over the front of my car, and pulled the flyer away so it wouldn't rip. I thought it was going to be another party invitation, but it wasn't. It was a missing person's report about a high school student named Ruth-Ann Summers who had gone missing a few months earlier. It had been all over the news since it happened, and a chill swept up my spine. I still couldn't imagine how a girl could disappear in broad daylight from the middle of campus like that.

Folding the flyer in half, I moved to put it in my pocket but felt a sharp pain in my neck. My vision started to blur and when I lifted my hand to touch the spot in my neck, my arm grew limp. My heart pounded as a pair of hands wrapped around my rapidly numbing body. Fear coursed through me, and I tried to yell for help, but the words were stuck on the tip of my tongue. They lodged in my throat as everything faded to black.

—–∿∿–—

The instant the fog cleared my head, I became aware of the cold. It was almost numbing, and there was a horrible smell all around me, as if maybe a sewer line had erupted nearby. Out of habit, I reached out with my left hand for my phone, but there was nothing there except the feeling of a bare mattress. I opened my eyes slowly, and was startled when I saw nothing but darkness. I lifted my hand in front of me to gauge my vision, but I couldn't even see it.

Sitting up, I felt a tug at my right ankle and moved my hand down my leg to find a cuff of some kind wrapped around it. It was not a normal handcuff, but thick and heavy, and I gasped when I felt a chain connected to it. Following it with my hands, I reached its end, where it was welded to a metal plaque that seemed to be bolted to the wall.

My body began to shake as I sat on the floor, pulled my knees to my chest, and wrapped my arms tight around them. I bit down hard on my bottom lip to hold back the sob that threatened to erupt.

I'd been kidnapped.

Tears began to slip down my cheeks as I sat in the cold, wondering what was going to happen to me. I waited, praying that my abductor wasn't still around, and tried to take deep breaths, calming breaths, but all that seemed to do was get me more upset. The last thing I needed, though, was to pass out *again*. I wiped my face and cleared my throat, unsure if what I was about to do was a smart idea.

"Hello?" I said, my voice shaking. "Is anyone there?"

Just as I started to feel some measure of calm with the idea that I was alone, a rattling noise sent my heart flying again. I stood and shook as I looked from left to right, straining to hear anything else. A sniffle broke the silence.

"Hello?" I said again, trying to steady the quiver in my voice. Now that I was standing, I could see a soft sliver of light around what must have been a door. I stepped forward, pulling at the chain around my ankle and trying to get closer, but it was just out of my reach. "Please, can someone hear me?"

"What's your name?" a soft voice answered.

I moved toward the wall to my left, from where the sound came. "Lillian. Lillian Locke, but you can call me Lee if you'd like. What's your name?"

"Anna," she said, barely above a whisper.

"Hi, Anna. It's really great to hear your voice. Do you know where the hell we are?" I asked, walking back to where the chain connected to the wall and gave it a strong pull. It was a relief to know I wasn't alone, but I needed to find a way out of here.

"No, I don't. Do you know what day it is?"

"Um . . . it was October first, I think. Or it could be the second by now, I can't tell."

I looked around. The walls were made of wood, but they did not seem thick when I pushed against them. I put my ear to one to see if I could hear anything, but there was nothing. Glancing up, the ceiling appeared to be made of wood, too, and I could faintly make out what looked to be a vent at the top of one of the walls. It had some sort of mesh over it, which must have been why I could hear Anna so well. I sighed and slammed my chain against the floor before sliding down to sit on the thin carpet. I tried to hold back the new wave of tears that threatened as I realized I was locked up tight in this makeshift cell.

Has anyone noticed I'm missing yet? I was supposed to call or text Richard by now, or maybe it's late and Emma has called my family to try and find me.

My hands shook as I ran them over my hair and body, checking to see if there was anything wrong with me. Other than my hair being tangled, I was just relieved that it hadn't been chopped off or shaved or anything crazy like that. I was still wearing the clothes I remembered putting on the last time I got dressed—a simple blue, long-sleeved sweater, jeans, and my running shoes. The only thing I seemed to be missing was my jacket, and that would have been handy right now. I couldn't believe how cold it was.

"How long have you been here?" I asked Anna.

"Six months," Anna said, after a long pause.

Another voice soon followed. "Two months," it said.

My jaw dropped and my eyes brimmed with new tears when the second voice spoke up.

"Five months," a third voice quavered.

I whimpered and covered my mouth with both hands when yet a fourth voice answered. "Two months."

Oh God, oh God, oh God, oh—

The last voice could barely be heard. "Me, too."

My body shook as I tried to wipe the tears streaming down my cheeks. "H—How many of you . . . are down here?"

"Six now," Anna whispered. "We would have had seven, but Nina didn't make it. You are in her room now."

Nina? I knew that name. Nina . . . Nina Ro—something or other. I think I saw that name on a flyer, too, just like the one about that Ruth girl.

"Anna, what's your last name? All of you, what are your names?" I asked.

"Anna Lin."

"Kandace Veccio."

"Linda Baker."

"Sara Turner."

"Ruth-Ann Summers."

My heart pounded as images of each of their flyers flashed in my head when they said their names. They were all still alive. All but one. So many assumed they had already been murdered, but they were here. And now I was one of them.

A tear slid down my face thinking about my mother, brother, and Emma. They were going to be sick with agony. And Richard! He would go insane when he found out I was gone.

Bile rose in my throat as I remembered the worried look in his eyes the last time I had seen him. A wave of anxiety took hold when I thought of what he would be going through. That he might have to be the one to call my family and tell them I was missing.

"Stop it, Lee. Focus," I whispered to myself.

Closing my eyes, I took a deep breath through my mouth and let it slowly exhale through my nose. I did that until I felt my heart start to slow back to its normal pace. Feeling better, I racked my brain to try and remember if I had been pushed into a car or carried off somewhere, but the only thing I could remember was reading the missing person's flyer . . . and then black.

"Shit, I cannot remember how I got here."

"It's the drugs," someone said.

"What drugs? And who said that?"

"He sneaks up behind you and stabs you with a needle that knocks you out. And it's Ruth."

"He? Who is he? Do any of you know him?"

"No," Ruth answered.

"But I don't remember even seeing a guy."

"It's how he got all of us," Anna said through the wall between us. "In time, you will remember."

Coughs and the occasional sniffle filled the void of silence, and it began to make me nervous.

"Where are you all? Do you all have your own rooms?" I asked, wanting to change the subject.

Anna was the one to answer again. "I'm kind of in the middle. You're in the room to my right, and Sara is to my left. Across from your room is Ruth. Linda is across from me, and Kandace is across from Sara. We haven't left our rooms since we got here."

"I remember all of you from the news," I admitted. "Ruth especially. You just graduated from high school, didn't you, Ruth?"

"Yeah. I got taken a week after my eighteenth birthday."

"So what does this asshole want with us?"

"Sex," several voices said at once.

"What!"

My heart fell to my stomach as I let that shocking piece of information sink in. I felt my skin start to heat up with the amount of rage that was boiling inside my body. I started feeling around the room for something, *anything*, to take my anger out on. All I could find was a plastic-covered mattress and a large bucket that I now realized was the source of the stench in this room.

"Are you fucking serious?" Standing, I picked up the bucket and threw it across the room. "I'm going to fucking kill him! I'm going to wrap my hands around his neck and squeeze until his eyes pop out of his head!"

"Will you shut up?" one of the girls yelled. "If he hears you and comes down here, I swear I'll tell him it was you."

I whipped my head in the direction of the noise, my eyebrows shooting up in shock. "Excuse me?"

"Lee, Kandace is right. Please be quiet," Anna said, her whisper urgent. "If he hears us, we'll all suffer. You have to trust us when we say you do not want that."

The fear in her voice caused me to start crying again. "What do you mean 'hears us'? Are we in his home?"

"We don't know. He leaves us alone a lot. Sometimes for hours, but other times . . ."

"How can you guys just sit here and not do anything? Have any of you tried to escape?"

It was Kandace again. "Yeah, let's ask Nina how that worked out for her? Oh, wait, we can't. She's fucking dead!"

"Kandace, please," Anna said, hushing her. "Lee is going through what all of us went through when we got here."

"Went? What do you mean, *went*? It's not past tense, Anna. I'm still going through this shit."

A noise above our heads caused Kandace to fall silent. I looked up at the sound of footsteps, my heart racing. There was a pause and then the click of locks turning, at least five of them, before a door creaked open and more footsteps thundered down what must have been the stairs. I held my breath and moved as far back into my room as I could until my back hit the wall. A much thicker sounding door scraped open and shut. The hinges must have been rusted over because I wanted to cover my ears from the piercing sound it made.

Another lock turned, causing me to jump as its echo reverberated around the room.

"Are my girls being bad?" a taunting voice asked.

My hand came over my mouth to cover a whimper as he swished his keys around.

"Are my girls yelling?" His voice grew nearer, and tears continued to fall down my face. "You know how I hate my girls misbehaving."

My eyes were glued to the small slit of light above the door. I slid down the wall and pulled my knees tight to my chest. I was shaking, almost dry heaving, by the time a shadow appeared in front of my room.

"Lilly," he whispered. "Have you been stirring up my girls?" I shut my eyes tight when something scratched against the outside of my door, followed by a moan. "Maybe I should give you a preview of what's to come."

It didn't escape me that he had called me Lilly. Very few people in my life called me that anymore. I hated it, because it reminded me of being a four-year-old.

Keys jingled as he unlocked the door and pushed it open. Faint light spilled into my dark room, creating a halo around a tall man. I couldn't make out his features but I could feel he was waiting for a reaction from me. Unfortunately for him, I was frozen, unable to do anything but sit there in complete and utter fear. After a minute of silence, he turned and unlocked another door across from me, and I heard Ruth cry out.

Angry at the thought of what I knew he was about to do, and having him say he was going to do that to me, too, I got up and ran for the open door. I didn't get too far and was stopped when the chain pulled at my ankle, which caused me to fall face first to the ground.

"You fucking coward!" I yelled. "She's just a child."

"Yeah, but she swallows like a pro," he chuckled, keeping his back to me. "Don't worry, Lilly, you will get your turn soon enough."

All I could do was lie there and cry, refusing to look up and watch, as a mix of moans, whimpers, and grunts resonated around me. I had to cover my ears when I heard him slap Ruth, yelling at her to stop crying. *Please, God, why are you doing this to me? To any of us?* I swore to myself if he tried that with me, I'd fucking bite it off.

Chapter 2

Day Two

I must have cried myself to sleep, because when I woke up there was a small light on above my head. I was still on the floor and ached all over from crying so hard all night. I rubbed my eyes, trying to get them to adjust to the harsh fluorescents, and gasped when I saw two large hiking boots in front of me.

"Good morning, Lilly."

I scooted back against the corner of the room, turning my head away while watching him from the corner of my eye. "Don't touch me," I said, feeling my body tense from the stress of fear pulsating all throughout my body.

"Oh, I plan on doing a lot more than just touching you," he said, laughing. "I have big plans for us."

"Why are you doing this to me?"

"Because I chose you." He walked forward and squatted in front of me.

He had on thick jeans that were faded and stained, and a black leather jacket. His boots were caked in mud, with a broken-off pine needle sticking out from one, which told me we were probably out in the middle of nowhere. I raised my eyes to scan his face and was surprised at how young he looked. Late twenties, maybe a little older if I had to guess. His brown hair was short, almost military cut, and his eyes were a deep brown, almost black.

"You are so beautiful," he whispered, lifting his hand and running his fingers across my arm. "A wonderful addition to my harem."

I stood up and went to move away, but he followed my actions and pressed his body against mine.

"I said, don't touch me."

Gripping my arm tight, he pushed his hips against my body and thrust. "You're in no position to tell me what to do."

I jerked my arm away and spun around, spitting in his face. "I'm not some fucking blow-up doll, asshole. I'm a person! I have parents, friends . . . a boyfrien—"

I was silenced with a slap across the face. Grabbing me around my neck, he lifted me off the ground. I raised my hands and tried to push him off but that seemed to cause him to tighten his hold.

"Let's get one thing clear, little girl. I own you! You belong to me until I am bored with you." The smell of beer and cigarettes was strong with every word he sneered at me. "You have no parents, no friends, and no boyfriend. Understand?"

I couldn't answer him. His palms were pushing so hard against my throat that it took everything in me not to black out. He let go of me, and I dropped to the floor with a gasp. Turning his back to me, he walked toward the open door, laughing.

My mind reeled with anger and disgust as I watched the cocky bastard walk away from me. Who did this guy think he was? Forget my family, boyfriend, and friends? *Oh, hell fucking no!* I coughed and braced my hands against the floor, pushing myself up.

"My name is Lillian Locke," I said, stopping him in his tracks. "My mom's name is Sadie, and my brother's name is Noah. My best friend is Emma, and my *boyfriend's* name is Richard." It felt good saying their names, even though I knew I would pay for it later.

He took a deep breath and continued to the door. "How sad for you, and to think I thought you were a smart person." He turned and faced me. "Maybe I should go pick up that best friend of yours and put her mouth to work down here. She's not exactly my type, but I can make an exception."

"You bastard! If you touch—"

"You'll do what? Look around and accept that this is your life. Let's see if a day or two without food will help that sink in."

I listened as he locked the door behind him and turned off the light, surrounding me in darkness once again. I waited to hear the cries of another, thinking he would brutalize one of them, but he didn't. I heard him open the thick door, shut it, and head back up the wooden steps.

—∿∿—

Forty-Eight Hours Missing
—Richard

"Have you called Sadie and Noah yet?"

"Of course I called them! What am I, an idiot?" I paced the length of Lee and Emma's living room, clutching my cell phone, willing it to ring and be Lee on the other end.

Emma sniffled, still in tears. "Calm down, Richard. We can't fall apart now. We have to keep calm."

Berating myself when my sister's voice cracked, I stopped pacing and sat down, pulling her into my arms. "I know. I'm sorry. I shouldn't have snapped like that."

Emma nodded against my chest as she continued to cry. Over the top of her head, I saw our older brother, Luke, watching us with worried eyes. He was stationed in front of the television, where he'd been since Emma called to tell him Lee was missing.

I looked away, needing a moment to let out a breath and calm down. I never would have met Lee if it hadn't been for Luke. He'd come to CU on a sports scholarship when I was still in high school. He blew out his knee the next year, but I was hooked on Colorado the first time our parents brought us to visit him. The smell, the mountains, the girls—I was in heaven. I applied to two colleges when the time came: CU and San Diego. When I got my acceptance letter, Luke and I started looking for places to move in together.

A year later, Emma joined us. She and Lee met freshmen year and moved into a small apartment together the next fall. Like a good brother, I'd volunteered to help them move, and it was love at first sight. Lee had been wearing a pair of running shorts and a matching top, both of which had her high school track team name and an image of a knight's helmet—the mascot—on them. She was tiny, like my sister, but had an air of confidence about her that drew me in. Her golden blond hair and blue eyes both shone. She was easy-going, strong, and organized. I was surprised how at ease I felt around her, and spent half the day wondering how I'd never met her before then.

It had taken me the next year to gather the nerve to ask her out, but being with her had been a dream come true ever since.

"Richard . . . Richard?"

I shook myself out of my daze and looked at Luke, who had tapped my shoulder.

"Sorry, Luke, spaced out for a second."

He pointed behind him and I glanced over his shoulder to see Lee's brother, Noah, standing just inside the front door.

He was as grim as the rest of us. His short blond hair stuck out in every direction, as if he had just gotten out of bed, and his blue eyes were red-rimmed and bloodshot.

"Noah." I walked over to him and shook his hand. His grip was weak and he smelled like he hadn't showered in days, reeking of coffee and cigarettes. "Any news?" I asked, looking over at Emma who had moved to the couch.

"The police still have her car and belongings, checking them for prints and so on. Aside from that, I have nothing."

"Boulder County residents and students at the University of Colorado Boulder are stunned and terrified tonight as another girl has disappeared from campus without a trace." All of us turned our heads to the television just as a picture of Lee flashed across the screen. *"Lillian Locke, a twenty-year-old athlete and Eldorado Springs native, was last seen walking to her vehicle on Tuesday, October 1st, around one thirty in the afternoon."*

Noah walked to the small coffee table in front of the television and sat down, his eyes still glued to the screen.

"This now brings the total number of missing girls to seven, and has prompted state officials to seek the assistance of the Federal Bureau of Investigation in their search for the person, or persons, responsible. Twenty-year-old Anna Lin, twenty-one-year-old Kandace Veccio, nineteen-year-old Linda Baker, twenty-one-year-old Sara Turner, twenty-two-year-old Nina Rosado, and recent high school graduate, eighteen-year-old Ruth-Ann Summers, who came to the university on a high school tour two months ago, are all believed to have been abducted within two miles of the CU Boulder campus." Pictures of each girl flashed across the screen as their names were called.

"University and city police are still asking that all women walk to and from classes in groups, and be especially cautious when going out at night. University officials are also reminding students and faculty to wear rape

whistles, provided free of charge, and to report any suspicious activity to authorities immediately. A press conference will be held at the university this evening for students and parents who have any questions regarding what the school is doing to prevent this tragedy from happening again. This is Carrie Voss, live from the Boulder campus, back to you in the studio."

I looked at Emma. "You are not going anywhere without one of us with you until this asshole is found. Do you understand me?"

"But—"

"No buts," Luke said. "Richard's right. I don't care if you are just walking to your car to get a pack of gum. You are not going out alone."

"I agree, Emma." We turned to see Adam Quinn, Emma's boyfriend, standing by the front door. "There is no arguing over this." Adam was quick to join my sister on the couch and wrap his arms around her. "I know you're scared, and love to argue, but please don't fight us on this. Okay?"

I turned away when Emma agreed with Adam, leaning in to kiss him just as Lee's brother stood up and walked out the door.

Wanting to talk to Noah without an audience anyway, I followed him out into the apartment parking lot where he lit a cigarette, taking a long drag. He held the pack out for me and I took one. I hadn't smoked in a year—I'd quit when Lee expressed her hatred for them—but at the moment it seemed just the thing to calm my nerves.

Noah was staring off into space when he spoke. "I'm going to poke my nose around BPD headquarters and see what they have to say. Campus police got all bent out of shape when I asked to see their files."

I nodded, trying not to get my hopes up. Noah was a police officer in Eldorado Springs, and had been for almost ten years. That was a small town, though, and Boulder was a whole different ball game.

"I'm going to take Luke with me to check out this press conference at the school. See what they have to say."

"That's a good idea," Noah said.

I sat down on the curb, resting my head in my hands. Noah sat next to me, and when he set his hand on my shoulder, I lost it.

"My Lilly is a smart girl, Richard. If she's still . . . she will give us time to find her."

"That's what I'm afraid of." I sniffled and wiped my eyes. "What would she allow herself to go through just to—"

Noah reached over and squeezed my shoulder.

"Whatever she needs to, bro."

Chapter 3

Day Three
—Lillian

I woke up to the sound of Patsy Cline's "I Fall To Pieces" blaring around me. It was eerie how it echoed through the walls. Her voice sounded so depressing and broken, just like us. It also seemed to be on repeat, and after the fourth time listening to it, I almost screamed for him to shut that shit off.

"Anna, are you there?"

"Where else would I be?"

"Sorry. So what's up with the song?"

Kandace, who seemed to always respond abrasively and with little tact, decided to answer. "He plays it all the time, and it's annoying as fuck!"

There was a moment of silence between all of us as we listened to the song repeat over and over words of loneliness and heartache. It was his way of fucking with us; I got that. It didn't make it less upsetting.

"I didn't get my period again," Anna said.

"Me either," someone whispered. I was almost certain it was Ruth.

"Shit." *I gotta get out of here.* "It might just be stress or lack of food. Try not to think about it."

"Lee, I'm pregnant," Anna said, her voice breaking.

"Are you sure?"

"Trust me, I'm sure."

This flipped a switch in me. I shouldn't have been surprised. I doubted the asshole was strapping on a rubber when he came down here, but it added to the constant waves of fear, anger, and revulsion that seemed to course through my body ever since I'd gotten here. Saliva started filling my mouth and I was quick to move in the direction of where I knew my bucket was, but I somehow held the bile down.

"So is that what you want, you sick fuck?" I shouted, after spitting the fluid out of my mouth and into the bucket. "To have us as your own sex slaves so you can breed? Sorry to tell you, jackass, but I'm on the shot. So you're not getting me pregnant anytime soon."

"He's not here, Lee," Linda said over me. "He plays the music when he leaves and turns it off when he gets back."

"Well, isn't that just peachy?" I said, and sat on my mattress. "I hope he gets struck by lightning."

"We can pray," Anna said.

"Yeah, and then we can all die from hunger," a voice I thought might have been Sara spoke next.

"I'm surprised he remembers to feed us at all. Well, feeds you all. I haven't eaten anything since I've gotten here."

"Lee, when he was in your room, you said something about having a boyfriend. What was his name again?" Anna asked.

I couldn't help the smile that spread across my face at the mention of Richard. That always seemed to happen when I thought of him, or if someone brought him up.

"Richard," I answered. "His name is Richard."

"So tell me about Richard," Anna said. "How long have you two been together?"

"For a little over a year, but we were friends for a year before that." I smiled a little, letting the memory of him wash over me. The second I met Richard, I knew he was going to be the one for me. It was like I felt whole when he was around. "He is the most amazing man I've ever met."

"What does he look like?" Ruth asked.

"He's got shaggy, dark brown hair and blue eyes. He's from California, so tall and fit, and has this permanent tan that makes me jealous every time he takes his shirt off." I couldn't help but laugh at myself with that last comment. Richard always made fun of me because I burned so easily. "He's got a great smile, and an even better sense of humor. Sometimes I feel like he's too good to be true. He always does these little things to make me feel special. Like, no matter how far apart our classes are, he runs across campus just to walk me to my next class." I felt the tears starting to brim my eyes. "I never got to tell him that I loved him."

"I'm sure he knows, Lee," Ruth said. "Guys just know those kinds of things. My boyfriend, Troy, just came up to me one day and said, 'I love you, too.' I never even told him that I loved him, but he already knew, and he just wanted to say it back."

"That's sweet, Ruth. Sounds like a nice guy."

"Can we please not talk about this?" Kandace said suddenly.

Sara spoke up then. "Oh, shut up, Kandace. I want to hear more."

"Me, too," said Ruth.

"So, Lee, was he any good in bed?" Linda asked with enthusiasm.

"Linda!" four separate voices cried.

"What?" Linda laughed.

Kandace groaned. "Of all topics you have to bring up down here."

"So what? We're not getting anything good down here anyway." Linda sighed. "Might as well hear about when we did."

"I never want to have sex ever again if I get out of here," Ruth said.

"Ruth, what you're going through is not sex," I replied. "What *he* is doing to you is rape. When you care about someone with all your heart, sex can be the best thing you have ever felt."

"I know. I almost did it once, with Troy, but . . ."

"You weren't ready?" I asked.

Ruth sighed. "No. I thought I was ready, and I do love him, but I just got scared when we tried." There was a short pause before Ruth let out a loud cry. "I hate that *he* was my first. I would give anything to have had that moment with Troy, but now I'll have to live the rest of my life with the memory of that disgusting *thing* inside me."

I let that soak into my brain for a while. I was lucky, and always would be, because I never regretted Richard being my first. There was no hesitation, blinding pain, or fear when Richard and I made love for the first time. It was perfect. And I felt so bad that Ruth had that moment taken from her.

"We are all going to need some serious therapy if we ever get out of here," Sara said.

"No shit," Anna responded, and we all laughed.

Suddenly the music stopped, and we fell silent when we heard his footsteps over our heads. I could hear the locks being turned and the sounds of his footsteps coming down the stairs. I covered my ears as the squeaky door opened and shut. I scooted my back to the corner of the room when I heard the jingling of keys echo through the hallway.

"Eenie, meenie, miney, moe. Who will be the first to go?" My heart stopped when the light for my room turned on. The door swung open, and I stood up, ready to fight. "Time to break in the new girl."

The look of sheer delight plastered across his face as he walked toward me almost made me gag.

Remember, Lee, don't scream, don't scream, don't scream.

The mantra continued to echo inside my head as he slapped me across the face, and I fell on top of the mattress, crying out in shock at his strength.

I bit down on my lip so I wouldn't scream; I'd rather die than give him the satisfaction. I fought back, kicking at him, but he caught my ankle and kicked me in return. The harder I fought, the harder he hit. After a while, he took both my wrists in one of his hands and held them over my head. A whimper almost escaped my lips when he ran his tongue from my neck to my ear.

"For such a mouthy little thing, you sure seem to suck at expressing yourself at the moment," he said, moaning and rubbing his groin against my crotch. "But I'm not worried. I'm always up for a good challenge."

I turned my head to the side when I felt him start to rub himself back and forth against me with a little more enthusiasm.

Don't think about it, Lee. Think of something else.

I tried to remember shopping trips with Emma, dinner dates with Richard, going hiking with my brother, but as soon as I did I was pulled back into the present by the disgusting noises he was making as he moved over me. I shuddered and he laughed.

"You like it when I moan, don't you?" he asked, reaching underneath my shirt and gripping my breast hard. "You're such a little slut." He pinched my nipple roughly, and I shut my eyes to keep from crying out. Without warning, he moved away from me and ripped his belt off. "You think you're strong?" he yelled, striking me with the belt buckle. I rolled over to my side and covered my head and face. "You think I'm being hard on you now?" he screamed, striking me again. I couldn't stop the tears at this point. They came out in buckets with each strike. "You haven't seen nothing yet, you stupid bitch!" he screamed again, striking me over, and over again.

Three Days Missing
—Richard

The press conference at the university turned out to be pointless. Luke and I sat there for two hours listening to the campus police give a speech about strength in groups and hotline numbers. By the time we'd gotten back to the girls' apartment, Emma and Adam were passed out on the couch. Too upset to sleep myself, I'd told the guys to go home and sent my sister to get some rest while I stayed up to wait for any news from Lee's brother. At some point, I must have fallen asleep because I was woken up at six in the morning by a knock at the door.

I got up, stretching my legs, and rubbed my hands over my face to help wake myself. With an average of just a couple of hours of sleep a night, my body was beginning to feel the effects. I opened the front door to find Noah, looking downright exhausted, on the other side.

"Any news?" I asked, yawning and running my hands through my hair.

He wouldn't look at me, and my heart sank as I saw he had been crying. "What? What is it?"

"I need you to come with me."

I felt a sick twist of dread in my stomach. "Please, just tell me now."

"I can't," he said, trying to mask his quivering voice. "I just need you to come with me right now. Okay, bro?" He looked up at me, and I could see the pain in his eyes. I nodded, grabbed my jacket, and followed him down the stairs toward his car.

"Where are we going?" I asked once we got on the road.

"Gold Hill."

"Where the hell is Gold Hill, and what's there?"

"An answer, and it's about thirty minutes away," Noah replied simply.

When we pulled up to the small brick police station in a town that seemed a minute long, there was a man standing outside, surrounded by multiple Government-marked cars.

"It's good to see you again, Officer Locke," the man said, shaking Noah's hand.

"I appreciate the phone call, Evan. And please, there is no need to be formal," Noah said, clearing his throat and motioning in my direction. "This is Richard Haines, Lee's boyfriend. Richard, this is Evan Davis."

I extended my hand to Evan and gave his a firm shake. He was older, maybe in his late forties, with a head that reminded me of Mr. Clean. He was at least a foot shorter than me, which made me feel even taller than I usually did at six feet.

Instead of walking toward the front of the building, Davis took us around back. "I'm sorry for what you two must be going through. I'll try to make this as fast as possible." He punched a few numbers onto a keypad and opened a thick metal door. Confused and annoyed, I followed the two men down a flight of stairs and into the basement. I stopped when I read the words *CORONER'S OFFICE* on the wall.

"Noah, what the fuck is going on?"

He stopped and looked at me. "They found a body, but the face was beaten so badly that she's unrecognizable. The FBI is down here taking evidence, pictures, and following protocol step by step, but you know Lee in ways we don't. Davis is going to see if they'll allow you to identify the body. There's no need to look at her face, *just* her body."

"Can't they just run fingerprints?"

Noah grew annoyed and walked right up to me, his nose inches from mine.

"I wouldn't ask this of you if that was a possibility, but it's not. The body doesn't . . . have any fingers. The bastard cut the victim's hands off." He grabbed my shoulders and pushed me against the wall, whispering with urgency, "If that's our Lee in there, then don't you want to know?"

He was right, I did want to know. I took a deep breath, squared my shoulders, and followed Noah toward the door marked *Morgue*. The hallway was dark and cold, with nothing but a depressing gray color on the walls and fixtures. I couldn't imagine working in a place like this. And the smell. It reminded me of antibacterial gel, Lysol, and death. Davis pointed to a group of chairs against the wall and asked us to sit and wait.

"What about DNA?" I asked when he'd disappeared inside. "Can't they just run yours against whoever is in there to see if they match?"

"That takes days. I want to know now."

Noah wouldn't look at me, his eyes fixated on the door that Davis had walked through, and I realized then what this moment really was. Today I might be identifying the dead body of the woman that I love.

Nausea and fear ripped through me as I leaned my head back against the wall and tried to steady the rapid beating of my heart. Could I do this? Was I ready to face my worst fears?

Before I could answer those questions, Davis came out with a sad expression on his face.

"I'm sorry, Noah, but they said no one who isn't part of the investigation can come view the body. They're worried about compromising the evidence."

"That's bullshit!" Noah stood and kicked his chair down the hall. "I'm not going to wait days to find out if my sister is dead."

"Again, I'm sorry—" Davis began to say, but was cut off when a female FBI agent stepped out, holding a camera in her hands.

"Is there a problem, gentlemen?" she asked.

"Yeah, there's a problem. I want to know if that's my sister in there!"

The woman was young, I would guess in her early thirties, medium height with long dark hair pulled back into a ponytail.

"I apologize Mr.—"

"Locke," Noah answered. "My name is Noah Locke, and I'm a police officer. A member of the service, just like you." I watched as he stepped forward and covered his hands over hers, which were still holding her camera. "And I am asking . . . no . . . begging you to just allow my family and me to find out if that is my baby sister in there. Please. If the roles were reversed, and you were standing where I am, I'd do it for you."

I got up and stood next to Noah, placing my hand on his shoulder, looking the woman in the eyes as her gaze shifted from Noah's to my own.

"Please," I said, silently praying she would give us this chance.

The woman looked torn as her eyes moved between Davis, Noah, myself, and her camera.

"I—I can't let you in, but I can take her picture and show it to you," she finally said. "Did your sister have any tattoos, birthmarks, or scars that you know of that would help you identify if this is her or not?"

Noah turned to me with pleading eyes. "She didn't have any tattoos or marks that I know of."

I shook my head. "No, she didn't."

I turned my back to them and ran my hands over my face, mentally going over by memory every square inch of Lee's body. Every curve and soft stretch of skin flashed through my mind as I tried to think of something. Finally, I did.

A year earlier, Lee had been injured when we went hiking. She'd slipped on a rock and sliced the inside of her thigh. It took only five stitches, but had left an L-shaped mark once the stitches came out. I made sure to kiss it every time we made love.

I turned and looked at the small group behind me. "Yes, on the inside of her right thigh there should be a small scar. I'd know that scar anywhere if I saw it."

The woman nodded. "Give me a minute and I'll be right back."

Davis followed her in as Noah and I stood waiting at the door. With each passing second, I felt my breathing become more labored as a level of anxiety began to course through my body. I closed my eyes and clenched my fists, praying to anything that would hear me that this body wasn't her. That this wasn't my Lee.

"Mr. Locke?" I opened my eyes to see the young woman step out, her camera extended in her hands. Noah and I met her halfway as she turned the camera around, showing us the back display screen. "I took a picture of the victim's right thigh"—she pushed the arrows on the screen, zooming in the photo, showing nothing but a bruised and dirty leg exposed from under a white sheet—"and as you can see there are no scars or marks."

"There's nothing there," I said. "It's not her." I looked up at Noah, seeing a soft smile cross his lips.

"Are you sure?" he asked.

"Positive." I nodded. "That is not our Lillian in there."

"Oh, thank God," he said, his shoulders drooping as if the weight of the world had rolled off them.

After thanking the young woman, and Davis, we made our way back to the car with what I thought was a little more hope. I looked down at my watch and noticed that it was almost noon. It felt like we had been down there all day instead of just a few short hours. As we pulled away from the building, I turned to Lee's brother.

"Noah?"

"Yeah?"

"Don't *ever* do that to me again."

Noah only nodded, letting me know he heard me, as we made our way toward the highway.

Chapter 4

Day Four
—Lillian

When I came to, I had no way of telling what time it was, but I did wake up to hear that annoying song playing again. At least that let me know he wasn't here.

"Oh, my fucking back," I said, wincing and rolling over to my stomach.

"You okay, Lee?" Anna asked, tapping on the wall.

"Peachy keen, Jelly Bean." I sighed and sat up. "How long was I out?"

"All night," Ruth replied. "For a second there, I thought you were dead."

"Please, it's going to take more than an ass-whipping to kill me." I was surprised to see a paper bag next to my mattress. Opening it, I found a small juice box and half a sandwich. "Oh, what a prince," I said, pulling out the sandwich and taking a bite.

I groaned when the taste hit my tongue. I hated praising the asshole in any way, but it was the best peanut butter and jelly sandwich I'd ever had. I was so hungry I wanted to swallow the whole thing in one bite, but I forced myself to go slow. No point in eating it too fast just to have it come back up.

"So, Anna, how the hell are we gonna get out of here?" I asked, after swallowing my last bite and drinking half my juice.

Kandace laughed. "Honey, you might as well rub a lamp. There is no way to get out of here."

"Nina figured it out," I said in a very matter-of-fact way.

"Yeah, in a body bag," Linda replied.

"So then we figure out what she did wrong and not do it again," Anna said with a little enthusiasm.

"Does that mean you're in?" I asked.

"Hell, yes. I'm beyond ready to get out of here."

Sara apparently agreed. "Then let's get the fuck out of here!" she said.

"I'm in," Ruth added, with Linda saying the same soon after.

"What about you, Kandace?" I asked.

"Sure, why not? It's not like I've got anything better to do."

"So, Anna, you're next to me, right?" I pounded my fist against the left wall, waiting for a reply.

"Yep," she answered, pounding back. "And Sara is in the room next to me."

"And you said Ruth is right across from me?"

"You're right, Lee," Ruth agreed. "And Linda is to my right."

"And I'm on the other side of Linda," Kandace yelled.

I looked around to see what I had, and as usual it consisted of a bucket, mattress, four walls, my chain, and a carpeted floor.

"What are you thinking over there, Lee?" Anna asked.

I looked at the wall and an idea popped into my head. "How thick do you think these walls are?"

"Not too thick, I guess. Why?"

"Well they're not cement, or we wouldn't be able to push against the walls like we can, so I'm guessing they're just pressboard." I pushed all over the wall, listening for a weak spot. I noticed the lower I got, the easier it was to push. "You see that, Anna?"

"Yeah, what does it mean?"

I knelt on the floor and started pulling at the carpet in the corner. It pulled away from the floor with little effort, and I jumped for joy when I saw that it was only dirt below, but the best part was that you could see the bottom of the wall. "Anna, below the carpet is dirt, and the walls don't go underground."

"Are you suggesting we dig our way out?" Kandace laughed.

"Not out, just to each other."

"And have you forgotten our little leash problem?" Kandace sighed, moving her chain around loud enough to make a point.

"One problem at a time. Let me work on the chain thing while you guys just start digging."

"Where do we hide the dirt?" Ruth asked.

"In your bucket or mattress if you can," Linda answered. "At least it will block out some of the smell."

"Just not too much," I called out. "We don't want him to notice anything."

I looked down at my chain and scratched my head, grimacing and pulling my hand away. My nails were filled with gunk and dirt. I wanted a shower in the worst way. My skin was starting to itch from the amount of accumulated crap caked over it. All this did was energize my brain into trying to figure out a way to get the chain off.

How the fuck do I get you off?

The room fell silent when we heard the song stop. I closed my eyes and sighed. With all my heart I thought of everyone I loved, with the last face flashing by being Richard's. I held on to that image, tightly, wrapping it around me like a security blanket. It had become my routine every time I heard that song shut off.

"I love you," I whispered when I heard the jingling of keys coming down the stairs.

Four Days Missing
—Richard

Time seemed to stand still. Police detectives and FBI investigators began circulating in and out of the girls' apartment like flies after the discovery of the body in Gold Hill. It was confirmation, without anyone officially saying so, that the body had belonged to one of the missing girls.

Agent Chase, the man assigned to investigate the abductions, interviewed each of us for almost an hour. We went over everything with him, from what Lee was wearing the day she went missing, to what she had eaten for lunch, to where and when she had made the service appointment that she was supposed to have gone to when she left campus. These were things that we had already discussed with the police department when we filed the initial missing person's report, and I saw it as a big waste of time. They should have been out there looking for the guy who took Lee, not bothering her loved ones by asking the same questions over and over.

Lee's mom, Sadie, had taken a leave of absence from her job and began coming and going from the apartment as well. Before anyone even realized it, she had practically moved in and taken over the household. Cooking, cleaning, washing, she was doing it all. A few times Emma and I had caught her standing in Lee's room, crying, but we never said anything. We understood that she had her own way of coping with the situation, and the fact that she was with us seemed to help her. It was terribly difficult for me, though. With her long blond hair and slim figure, Sadie looked a lot like Lillian, especially from the back. It was hard on my heart to walk into a room and think I'd seen Lee for a split second, just to realize it wasn't her. It was never her.

Noah didn't seem to be taking things well either. Despite being relieved that it hadn't been Lee, he had become almost inconsolable once the body we'd seen was identified as Nina Rosado. To him, it was proof that whoever had taken Lee was not just a kidnapper but a killer, and we didn't have much time left to find Lee.

"I know I don't have to tell you the statistics, Richard."

"No offence, Noah, but please try to keep these feelings to yourself," I whispered. "I'm not going to have you upsetting everyone by saying such things."

"I'm sorry, I don't mean to—"

"I know," I said, nodding. "They just don't need to be hearing that, especially your mom."

"How is she holding up?"

"If cleaning is what she does when she's a mess, then she's hardly holding on." I lit a cigarette and took a long pull. "Were there any new leads after they looked at the body?"

Noah shook his head. "They took everything to a forensic lab. They won't know, or won't say, until the tests come back."

"I need to know this, Noah, and don't give me the CliffsNotes' version." I paused before taking a deep breath. "What did this psycho do to that girl?"

"Richard, I can't. I can't think about it again." Noah went to walk away, but I stopped him and swung him around.

"No, you don't get to keep this to yourself," I said, close to yelling. "I need to know! Six girls are still missing, Noah, and Lee is one of them. I want to know what that sick bastard is doing."

Tears fell from his eyes as he looked into mine. "He brutalized her in every way you could think of," he whispered. "And I'm sorry, Richard, but I don't have the stomach to spell out to you what, specifically, that means."

Then he removed my hand from his shoulder and walked away.

I stood there in agony for what seemed like hours, imagining all the things my beautiful girl could be going through. I could literally feel my heart squeezing in my chest. I didn't want to acknowledge the possibility that I might never see Lee again, but I couldn't help it, and the thought alone had me on the edge of sanity. I had to get away. I pulled my keys out of my pocket and ran toward my car. I had to get away from the apartment.

Chapter 5

Day Seven
—Lillian

"You fucking coward!" I screamed, banging against the wall. I could hear Anna crying out in pain as he continued to attack her. "You're such a spineless piece of shit."

"Oh, I love it when you talk dirty to me, Lilly," he said.

The mix between the cries, moans, and slapping almost made me vomit. I was pulling so hard on my chain that I could feel it cutting through my skin.

"Eat shit, minute man," I shouted, letting my emotions get the better of me. "You want dirty? Take this fucking chain off me and I'll show you dirty, you fucking cock sucker!" I began pacing back and forth, slamming my fist into the wall when I neared it, and wishing it could have been his face. "Just give me five minutes—five minutes to show you—"

My rant was cut off by a loud thud in Anna's room, and then a few slaps against the wall. I stopped pacing and put my ear against it, hearing his grunting.

"I'm gonna fuck you up till you bleed, Lilly. And it's gonna feel so good," he whispered.

"You first," I yelled back, slamming my fists against the wall. There were a few loud bangs against the wall again and then the sound of him pulling up his pants. After, he left the room, shutting Anna's door behind him. I was seething when I heard him sigh as he strapped on his belt. He came over and stopped in front of my door, and I just stood there, waiting for the next round against this prick.

"Promises, promises," he said, laughing.

"That's not a promise, it's a fucking guarantee, shit head!"

We were all silent as we listened to him. But instead of entering my room, he turned and walked up the stairs, leaving us in our dark solitude.

Anna's whimpers echoed around us as we waited for the music to start. Once it did, I knelt against the wall and wept.

"Anna, are you okay?" Ruth called.

"Just give me a minute," she answered, sounding like she was having a hard time catching her breath.

I went over to the corner of the room, lifted the carpet, and started digging. After a while I could hear Anna on the other side doing the same. I remained that way for a long time, digging silently, until she spoke.

"Thank you."

"For what?"

"He didn't finish—in me—because of what you said."

I leaned against the wall. "What do you mean, he didn't finish?"

"He went over to the wall and jerked off on it."

"Are you serious?" If I wasn't sitting already, I would have fallen over with shock. "God, he's such a sick fuck."

"What? What's going on?" Sara asked.

"The asshole jerked off on Anna's wall." I didn't know why I was laughing, but for some reason I found it to be hilarious.

All the girls started laughing while Anna continued talking. "It was kinda weird, though. He acted like . . . it was almost as if he liked it." She giggled. "Like, he liked you calling him all those names."

With that comment, I stopped laughing. *Shit, good job, Lee.* I sighed and banged my head against the wall.

"Lee, what's wrong?" Anna whispered, so the other girls couldn't hear.

He'd figured out that no matter how many times he beat me, I wouldn't cry out, crippling his ability to get his rocks off, but he knew it pissed me off that he hurt the other girls.

He's gonna go after them to get to me.

"Nothing."

"Are you sure?"

"Shouldn't I be asking you that question?" I asked with a sad smile.

She huffed as I heard her lean against the wall. "As sad as it is to say this, I'm used to it. I've been here the longest."

"I'm sorry."

"Don't be. You have given us hope, Lee. Without you, we would just be sitting here waiting to die."

It made me smile knowing that I was helping in some small way. We had become a sisterhood, all of us leaning on each other for comfort. He hadn't raped me yet, and I stressed *yet*, but I knew my time would come soon. Hearing the girls cry out in pain every day was my reminder. The reminder that it wasn't a case of if, but when.

"Lee?" Anna's voice rang out, pulling me from my daze.

"Yeah?"

"Look!"

I looked down and saw that she had dug enough to be able to stick a few of her fingers under the wall. I bent down and smiled, touching her small fingers.

She pulled them back and laughed. "I wish I had the words to say how awesome this feels."

"Me, too." I let a few happy tears fall. Coughing, so Anna couldn't hear the quiver in my voice, I said, "I hate to ask this, Anna, but were you able to feel for anything in his pockets? Anything we could use to get out of these chains?"

"No, and I hate that I had never thought of that, but . . . I do have these." I looked down to see her fingers push two bobby pins under the wall.

I couldn't help but laugh. "My chain doesn't have a lock on it, Anna. And even if it did, I would have no idea how to pick one."

"None of our chains do, but you never know when they could be useful, right?"

"What? What are you guys talking about?" Ruth asked.

"Anna gave me a pair of bobby pins." I smiled. "I guess that's the equivalent of going steady around here."

"You guys can reach each other already?" Linda asked.

"Yep, and Anna is in dire need of a manicure," I said, trying to lighten the mood.

"I'm so jealous," Ruth grumbled.

"Don't worry, sweet pea, we're almost there," Linda said with a smile in her voice.

I looked down at the two bobby pins in my hand and sighed. Besides stabbing the fucker in the eyes with these, what the fuck could I do with them?

—‑/\/\/‑—

Seven Days Missing
—Richard

Search parties had formed around the surrounding forest areas of Gold Hill after Nina's body was discovered. Agent Chase asked us if we wanted to participate, but that question was answered when Luke had to stop Noah from pulling his gun out on the guy. Fucking idiot. Luke should have let Noah shoot the dumb ass for asking such a thing. We all knew we wouldn't be able to handle it if we found Lee dead.

"Lee wouldn't want you to fail out, Richard," Emma said, being more persistent than usual. Luke, Emma, and Adam started going back to class, and tried to convince me that I should go, too, but I just couldn't.

"Seriously? You're gonna pull that card on me?" I yelled, walking over to the couch and sitting down.

"It might help distract you a little," Adam said. "Get you out of the apartment for a few hours out of the day."

"I don't want to be distracted, Adam, I want to be out there!" I pointed out the window to the few reporters who still mingled around the complex. "I want to be ransacking every damn house until I find her. How the fuck am I supposed to concentrate on anything but her?" I looked down and ran my hands through my hair, trying to keep my tears at bay. I needed to keep it together.

"I'm just saying—"

"No!" I stood up and walked to him so that we were inches from each other. "What if it was Emma?" I asked, pointing over his shoulder at her. "What if she had been taken? Would you be leaving for class right now or would you be here, chain smoking"—I let a tear spill over— "and praying that every time the phone rang it would be her voice on the other end?"

He gripped my shoulders and pulled me into a hug. I pulled at his shirt and held on for dear life as I finally let my walls fall, letting my sobs take over. I couldn't ever remember crying so hard before in my life. I could hear Emma in the background crying, too, and that just made me feel worse.

"Oh my God," Lee's mother whispered, dropping the plate in her hands. It shattered into a million pieces as she fell to her knees on top of the glass. "Not my baby," she said. "Not my little girl." Adam and I rushed to her, lifting her off the ground so she wouldn't cut herself.

"No, Sadie, no," I said, pulling her to me, and rocking her back and forth. "I just . . . needed a moment. We still haven't heard anything."

"Oh, thank God," she whispered, wrapping her arms around me and crying into my shoulder. I rubbed her back and apologized over and over for upsetting her, until her tears subsided. After a few minutes she pulled away, took my face in her hands, and gave me a playful glare. "Next time you need to take a moment, do it in the bathroom," she said. "Understand?"

"Yes, ma'am," I agreed, giving her a hug. "I'm sorry."

"I know."

After watching Sadie walk away, I turned to Emma and my heart fell from the look in her eyes. I reached for her and she rushed into my arms. It had been a long time since I'd held my sister this way, but these last couple of days had changed our relationship. It's sad that it had taken Lee going missing for that to happen. She buried her face in my chest and I stroked her long brown hair as tears escaped her eyes. "Em, please don't think for one second that I wouldn't be just as destroyed if it was you who were taken," I whispered, kissing her hair. "I love you with all my heart. Never forget that."

"I love you, too," she whispered with a sniffle. "Even when you don't think before you speak."

I had to laugh at that. Our mom always said that to us when we were growing up.

The front door swung open and Luke walked in. "That's what I'm talking about," he said, walking over to us and wrapping his arms around both of us. "Family hug!"

"Oh my God, Luke," Emma said. "Get off." We all chuckled, including Adam, who was now helping Sadie pick glass up off the floor.

"Richard." The soothing, familiar voice made me choke up, and I turned to see my mom and dad standing in the front doorway. My mom started walking toward me but I met her halfway, wrapping my arms around her.

"Richard, I am so sorry. We'll find her. I can feel it," she whispered, kissing my cheek. "Whatever you guys need. Money, private detectives, anything." She sniffled, pulling away and kissing my cheek. "It's yours."

"Thanks, Mom."

It was a little comforting to have my parents here. They loved Lee the moment they met her, so I knew they would help as best as they could. When she went missing, I called them as soon as I had gotten off the phone with Sadie. They had promised they would fly in from San Diego to help make sure everything that could be done was being done.

Emma and Adam went off to class after introductions were made and hugs were shared between Lee's mom and my parents. I hated that it took something like this to bring us all together for the first time, but I was glad we could be together just the same. Eventually, Luke took our parents to get settled at a hotel, and Sadie went in Lee's room to take a nap.

I walked to the back patio and pulled out my pack of smokes, lighting one and taking a hard pull. I smiled to myself, remembering a conversation with Lee about my smoking, as if it happened yesterday.

"I hope you have stock in mouthwash."

"Come on, babe, it's not that bad." I put out my smoke and faced her. *"I've already cut it back to three a day."*

"Three more than I would like." She crossed her arms and pouted. *"You know they say you give up seven minutes of your life with every pack."* She smiled and walked over to me, took the pack of cigarettes out of my pocket, and held them up. *"To think what we could do with those gained seven minutes."* She smirked, wiggling her eyebrows.

"Done," I said, taking my cigarettes out of her hand and throwing them over her patio. She giggled when I picked her up and tossed her over my shoulder.

"Richard Haines, what are you doing?" she squealed, smacking my butt.

"Making up for lost time," I answered, rushing into her room and shutting the door.

I took one last pull from my smoke and flicked it away. That same night she told me she loved me. She had been talking in her sleep, but she still said it, and being the idiot that I was, I never said it back to her.

Please, God, I prayed. *Let me be able to say it back to her.*

Chapter 6

Day Ten
—Lillian

"Lee . . . Lee . . ." Anna whispered, tapping on the wall, and waking me from my sleep. "Lee, wake up."

"I'm up," I answered, rubbing the sleep out of my eyes. "What's—" I stopped when I heard a struggling gasp, along with a loud grunt, outside my door. *Shit, it was Ruth.* "Fuck!"

Not her, not anymore. She's just a child. I said a little prayer in my head and took a deep breath, preparing myself for what I was about to do.

"Hey, you needle-dick son of a bitch. Why don't you pick on somebody your own size?"

"Oh, there she is," he said. "I was wondering when you'd join us." Ruth cried out when the sound of a fist meeting flesh echoed around me. It was loud enough to even make me flinch. "Don't worry, Lilly, I'm almost done here."

Ruth cried out my name when another smack hit her skin.

I took another deep breath and crossed the line. "You know why you can't get me to scream? Because you're not a real man."

A few seconds later I heard a door slam against a wall, and then mine swung open. I stood there with my fists clenched as he walked in, not even bothering to close the door behind him like he usually did. For the first time

I saw the eyes of one of my captive sisters. Ruth was in a room across from me. She looked so small and frail; her dress tattered, stained with dirt and blood; her long red hair tangled, and her pale skin covered in bruises and welts. Her red-rimmed eyes met mine for a brief second before I met the gaze of my attacker.

"What did you say, you stupid bitch?" he yelled, punching me in the face. It wasn't hard enough to make me fall, but it was hard enough to make me stumble back against the wall.

"Lee, stop! Please." Ruth sobbed.

I licked the blood off my lip and laughed, knowing that it would just piss him off more. "You heard me, minute man," I replied, spitting blood in his direction. "Only a *real* man can get me to scream." He lunged at me and wrapped his hands around my neck.

"You're dead, you stupid slut! Do you hear me? You're dead! You're fucking dead!"

I couldn't hear Ruth's screams over his yelling and my own heartbeat pounding in my ears. I clawed against his face until I felt my fingers graze his right eye. With as much force as I could muster, I plunged my thumb into it, causing him to cry out and drop me to the ground. I grasped my neck, coughing, gasping for air, while he stumbled toward the door. I watched him as he went back over to Ruth, hitting her with so much force that she fell to the floor with a loud thud and didn't get up.

He made his way back over to my room, and I could already see that his right eye was starting to swell.

"Well, don't you look pretty," I wheezed as I sat up against the wall, and laughed. "How does it feel to get your ass kicked by a girl, you piece of shit?"

"Kick this, bitch."

Before I could dodge, his foot swung out, kicking me in the head. Everything went black.

—◦◦◦—

I rubbed at my head, feeling like there was a sledgehammer pounding against it. I was nauseous and could feel dried blood sticking to my face. I tried to sit up but was so dizzy that all I could do was lift my head. "My kingdom for an Advil."

"Lee!" the girls all yelled, causing me to wince.

"Not so loud, please."

"Lee, Ruth's not answering," Anna cried. "She hasn't made a noise since he left."

"Shit." I sat up and gasped when I saw that my door was still open, but more than that, so was Ruth's. The light from the hallway was on, allowing me to see Ruth lying on the floor in the same position she was in when she fell. "I can see her!" I coughed, still feeling the effects from that asshole choking me.

"What do you mean you can see her?" Linda asked.

"I mean I can fucking *see* her! The dumb ass left our doors open." I crawled toward the door until my chain pulled at my ankle. I cleared my throat, struggling to get the words out. "Ruth? Ruth, honey, wake up!"

"Come on, Ruth," Linda shouted, banging on their adjacent wall. "Wake up, baby girl."

"Ruth! Wake up!" I said, calling out as loud as I could while clutching my dry throat. I couldn't tell if she was breathing, and the fact that she was still in the same position as before caused my tears to come to the surface. After a few more yells, I breathed a sigh of relief when she started to move. "Oh, thank God."

I sighed, standing up and swaying.

"Is she moving?" Kandace asked.

"Yes." I couldn't help the laugh of excitement that came out when she sat up. "Ruth, are you okay?"

"Yeah, I think so. I just feel—" She stopped in shock and looked at me. I knew it wasn't because she realized that her door was still open and that she could see me, but it was because her chain fell loose from around her ankle. "Holy shit."

"Holy shit," I agreed, nodding to myself.

"What?" Sara asked. "What is it? Are you two okay?"

"I'm not chained!" Ruth said as she stood up. Before I could stop her, she started walking toward me. From the darkness of the hallway, our abductor lunged out and grabbed her around her neck.

"No!" My voice cracked as I screamed when I saw the disgusting grin across his face.

"Nighty night, Ruth," he said, his voice a sneer.

For a second my eyes met Ruth's, and then I fell to my knees screaming when he snapped her neck. Her body fell to the ground halfway to my room, her right arm stretched out as if she was trying to reach me. I stayed sitting on the floor for I don't know how long, just looking at her lifeless body. Her eyes looked black and fogged over as they stared off into nothing. I hadn't even noticed *him* until he walked over to me and kneeled down so his eyes were level with mine.

"That one's on you, little girl." He smirked, tilting his head. "Remember that next time you go running your mouth off."

He stood up and laughed, grabbing Ruth's body by the hair, and dragging her away from my doorway. Looking at me one last time, he slammed my door shut, encasing me in my darkness. I sat there, stunned, as I listened to him drag Ruth's body up the stairs. I didn't let the tears fall until I heard him turn the music back on.

—m—

Ten Days Missing
—Richard

Noah called around nine in the morning, asking me to drive down to his house so he could go over a few things with me. It was a twenty minute drive away, but the way I drove I got there in less than fifteen. His two-story town home was small but comfortable. Memories of sitting in his living room, watching sports and eating dinner with him and Lee, filtered into my mind as I sat in his driveway. I couldn't help but wonder if any of us would be what we used to be once we found Lee. When I walked through his front door and into the kitchen, I stood in shock as I saw the kitchen table and counters covered with files and newspaper clippings.

"Hey, bro," Noah said, walking down the stairs with a beer in his hand.

"Hi." I was unable to take my eyes away from the sight before me. "What's all this?"

"Answers." He reached in the fridge and pulled out a beer for me. "Come sit. I have some things to show you." He handed me the beer and I sat in the other kitchen chair that wasn't piled with paperwork. He pulled out a picture of every girl who had been kidnapped from campus, and lined them up in front of me. "The agent on this case lied to me, saying that none of the girls have anything in common, that this guy must be choosing the girls at random."

"How do you know he's lying?" I asked, taking a drink of my beer.

Noah pointed at the photos and moved each of them a little closer to me. "Look at the pictures and tell me what you see."

I looked down at the pictures and saw . . . nothing. One girl was black, one was Asian, another could be Hispanic, and the others were all white. Blondes, brunettes, and a redhead. All beautiful young girls.

"I'm sorry, Noah, I don't see it," I said, sitting back in my chair.

He picked up the picture of Lee and shoved it in my face. "Look harder!"

I took the picture and gazed at it. I remembered when it was taken. It was last year on the track field. We had all come out and rooted for her, even my parents who were in town, and she won second place in the one-hundred-meter race. And then it hit me. I looked at all the pictures again, and each one of them had a girl in a uniform. A soccer player, cheerleader, lacrosse, track, softball.

"They're all athletes," I whispered to myself.

"And not just any athletes, but athletes that played on the field," he said, taking a drink of his beer.

"So you think it's an athlete?"

Noah shook his head. "No, but I think it's someone in the athletic department."

"And what makes you so sure?"

"Because that's where they've been looking since the fourth girl was taken." Noah stood up and walked over to the far counter, picking up a file. "Your brother played football, right?" he asked, handing me the folder.

"Just his freshman and sophomore year," I said, taking the folder from him and opening it. "He blew out his knee and couldn't play anymore."

It was why Luke was still in college. He had been in physical therapy for almost a year and ended up having to take some extended leave from school so he wouldn't fail out. He still had problems with his knee once in a while, but he found his calling at wanting to work in sports medicine.

"In that folder is a list of people who work in the athletic department. I need you and your brother to check out anyone who's new to the program."

"Why the new ones?" I asked, looking over the list that consisted of maybe twenty names. "And why us? Why can't you do it?"

"If this guy was someone who had been around for a while, there would have been more girls missing over a longer period of time. This guy has to be new, working there for maybe a little over a year." Noah took a long pull of his beer. "And if I go in there, I'm going to come off as a cop. This person, if there, will see me a mile away and be spooked. I can't risk them running off and killing Lee because I was being a cop. I wouldn't be able to live with myself. You and Luke know the department a lot better than any of us, and you'll know who to ask. Not to mention, you two are not cops.

This asshole might be aware when the cops are around, but won't think twice with students. Do you think the two of you can do this?"

I didn't know the department that well. I knew a few head coaches, due to Lee and Luke, but that was it. I wasn't going to tell Noah that—seeing how excited he was with this new revelation—but I'd try any leads at this point.

I looked at him and nodded. "I'll do whatever it takes, Noah. You know that."

He patted my back and smiled. "Thank you."

Chapter 7

Day Thirteen
—Lillian

After Ruth was murdered in front of me, I couldn't find it in myself to do anything but cry. Anna begged me to move my mattress closer to the wall where our hole was, so she could hold my hand, but I couldn't. All the girls tried to get me to talk, even Kandace, but I just didn't have the energy to care. *He* even seemed to notice that I wasn't talking anymore, and it pissed him off.

He tormented me with a description of everything he'd done to Ruth's body before he dumped it, but even then I just lay there. *My fault. My fucking fault,* I thought, as he knelt over me and reached for my body with dirty, calloused hands.

Part of me thought I deserved it. Whatever he was going to do to me, there was a large part of my brain that told me it was nothing in comparison to what he'd done to Ruth. I let him wrap one hand around my neck and did nothing when he reached for his belt.

After a while he kicked me hard, screaming at me to say something, to fight him. But I couldn't. I just rolled over, curled into a ball, and waited for him to finish. He spat on me, called me worthless, and told me I'd better wise up or I would be the next to go. I would have told him to eat shit a few days ago, but now I didn't care. Ruth's blood was on my hands. He may have killed her, but I was the reason. She didn't deserve that. She didn't deserve to receive my punishment, and that's what it was. It should have been my neck he snapped; it should have been my body that was dragged away.

It was my fault.

—⁓—

"Lee, please come over here," Anna whispered sometime later.

I was losing my days. When I closed my eyes to sleep I didn't know if I was sleeping for minutes, hours, or a whole day.

"Look, I can fit my whole hand through now."

I looked up and saw her hand waving at the base of the wall. And despite what had happened earlier, despite my guilt over Ruth's murder, I let myself smile. I crawled over and lay down on the floor, taking her pale hand in mine. I couldn't control the tears that started to fall when Anna's thumb stroked my fingers.

"I'm so sorry," I said, weeping. "God, I'm so, so sorry. It's all my fault."

"No," all the girls yelled.

Anna gripped my hand tight. "No, Lee, never think that. It's him, and the sick and twisted game he's playing."

"If I would have just—"

"Lee," Linda said, cutting me off. "I swear to God, if you blame yourself again I will kick your ass." There was a small pause before they all started laughing. "Well, whenever we get out of here, it will be the first thing on my to-do list," she said in a very matter-of-fact way.

"Oh, I doubt that," Sara said.

"I'm serious!" Linda replied.

"Really, Linda? The first thing?" Sara asked.

"Well, I'll kick her ass after I take a shower. Or maybe just smelling me will knock her out."

Even I had to laugh at that. We were some smelly girls.

"I don't know why you said shower, Linda. I plan on taking a nice warm bath," Kandace said.

Anna tugged on my hand. "What about you, Lee? What's the first thing you're gonna do when you get out of here?"

Still holding Anna's hand, I sat up and wiped the tears from my eyes. "I'm going to burn this fucking place down." I sniffed. "I just haven't decided if I want him in here or not when I do it."

"Why burn it?" Kandace asked.

"To get rid of the smell," I said, laughing. It felt good to joke around again. All the girls laughed with me, all except Anna. I felt her pull at my hand, and I knelt down so I could hear her better.

"Promise me, Lee, that we'll get out of here," she whispered. "Promise me you'll let me be here when you burn it down."

I put both my hands over hers and gripped them with determination. "I promise, Anna. I swear it. Or I'll die trying."

I kissed her hand and let go, needing to stand up and stretch. I rubbed at my sore muscles as the aches and pains radiated throughout my body. I looked down at my arms and could make out the dark bruises in the shape of handprints against my pale skin. It was a sickening reminder of him, ensuring that even when he was physically not here, we knew what we were to him. I wished that I could just rub dirt on them, masking them from my sight, but what was the point? No matter what I did they'd still be there. And even when they finally faded away, they'd still be there in my mind.

I walked around, dragging my chain and wondering how I was going to live up to my promise. It was getting colder, which meant snow was starting to fall. You would think being underground we would be well insulated, but every day I found myself pulling my arms through the sleeves of my thin sweater just so I could warm them up.

I dug my hands into my pockets to warm them when I came across the bobby pins Anna had given me. I twirled them between my fingers, allowing myself to get lost in my thoughts. I found myself singing along with the fucking annoying song that kept repeating upstairs while letting my mind wander as I stared at the metal plaque bolted to the wall. The end of my chain led right up to the center of it, where a link was sawn in half and welded to it. The plaque was at knee level and held up by four bolts, one on each corner that could have been unscrewed if I had a flat-head screwdriver. I sat down cross-legged, running my fingers over the plaque.

"Hey, Anna?"

"Yeah?"

"The plaque that holds your chain to the wall, can you describe it to me?" She described in full detail the exact same thing I was looking at. "Do all of yours look like that?" I yelled, and received confirmation from everyone.

"Why? What are you thinking?" Anna asked.

"Not sure, but I have an idea."

Then the music stopped, and there was a lot of ruckus overhead. He came down the stairs in a rush, opening and slamming the main door behind him. I hurried to the overturned carpet and flipped it back, covering the hole in the floor.

Sara whimpered as he unlocked her door. We could hear her being slapped around before he took off his belt. Whenever he came down here pissed off, he always went to her. I had started to see a pattern when it came to who he picked and why. When he was angry, he picked Sara; she always cried the whole time he raped her, and she was the one out of all of us who did. I think the sick fuck liked that more than anything.

With Anna, it was torture. She told me once that his favorite new thing to do was tape a ball to her mouth, because when he raped her she would vomit due to her pregnancy. I assumed he liked seeing her choke when he did it. Sometimes he would burn her, and I would scream and pound on the walls every time I heard him flip open his lighter.

When he was in a good mood, he picked Linda. If Linda didn't act like she was having sex with him, instead of being raped, he would hit her until she was unconscious. She said that was the hardest thing she'd ever had to do, to kiss him back, to pretend to moan in pleasure, and even sometimes to hold him afterward. The sick fuck.

And then there was poor Kandace. Kandace seemed to be his favorite. We all knew why; she even realized it, too. Kandace always fought back, and he loved it. You could hear her slapping and hitting him, but he would just laugh at her, throw her to the ground, and do whatever he wanted to her.

With me, I think it was just a pain thing. He hadn't tried to rape me. Not even once. Fondle, yes, but never rape. It seemed like he saw me as his own personal punching bag. A few times he'd come down here just to beat me and then leave. Even when he was here dropping off that pathetic bag of food, or emptying our buckets, he would have to beat me. I knew he liked me yelling at him, that was obvious, but I was pretty sure that wasn't why he had taken me. I wondered if my smart mouth had just been an unfortunate added bonus. To be honest, I wasn't sure what was worse, being raped or being beaten, but it was a question I hoped I never had to answer.

He laughed, hitting Sara again. "That's right, bitch, cry out!"

Feeling a little bit of my confidence returning, and wanting her to know we had her back, I started to sing.

"Oh, yes I am wise, but it's wisdom born of pain. Yes, I've paid the price, but look how much I gained."

I sang it so loud that my voice cracked at the end. While I continued singing the chorus to "I Am Woman"—the only part of the song I could remember—I turned my attention back to the plaque. With bobby pins in hand, I put my crazy idea to work.

Thirteen Days Missing
—Richard

For three days, Luke and I had been checking out every person on the list. Luke's old football trainer, Joe, helped us limit the list down to ten from the almost twenty that were there. Joe had been working for the athletic department for more than thirty years, so we felt comfortable going to him over anyone else.

We spent hours following these men around, unsure of what we were looking for but taking notes on everything from what car they drove to what brand of cigarettes they smoked. Noah would call every once in a while, just to see if we were making any progress, but I continued telling him that if we found anything he would be the first person we would call.

"I bet he's not getting anywhere on his end, and that's why he keeps calling you," Luke said. He was ready to move on from the guy we had been checking out. His name was Henry Castro, and we had been following him around for five hours. All he did was time the runners for their practices and write the time down on his clipboard. We made a copy of the list for Adam so he could look up the addresses of all the people Joe said were new. Adam was driving over to Henry's house to see if he seemed decent.

I felt my phone vibrating again, and was relieved to see that it was Adam.

"Hey, man, how's it looking?"

"Mr. Castro has a wife and three kids," he replied. "He lives in a nice little area, too. I'm sorry, man, but I don't think he's the guy."

"It's cool, Adam. I didn't think so either. So who's next on the list?"

"I want to check out this guy named Thomas Reed."

I looked down at my list and found the name toward the bottom. Joe had taken the time to write a few notes by each of the names, and by Thomas' name it said: *field department, working almost a year, seems nice, but doesn't talk much.*

"Where does he live?" I asked.

"Nederland."

"Where the hell is that?"

"About thirty minutes west of Boulder," he answered. "It's just past the

Barker Reservoir."

"So out in the boonies?" I laughed.

"Anything west of Boulder is the boonies to you," he said with a chuckle. "But that's why I want to check it out. This Thomas kid is the only person on this list who's from Colorado. Everyone else moved here for the job."

"You need Luke and I to tag along?" Luke heard me, and his attention seemed to perk up a little.

"No, but how about you give Noah a break from girl-sitting? Go eat some lunch. I'll call you if I find anything."

I hung up the phone, and Luke and I headed for the car. When we got to the apartment, Noah was chain smoking outside while the women were in the living room watching some annoying chick movie. Watching them sitting there on the couch made my heart ache. Sadie was sitting in the middle, with Emma to her left and my mom on her right. They both had their heads on one of Sadie's shoulders, and all of them were holding hands. They didn't even seem to be watching the movie, but were just using it as an excuse to be close to one another. I felt the tears start to rise when the phone rang. I walked over and answered it.

"Hello?"

"Hi, it's Agent Chase." He sounded very monotone, which made me nervous. Chase was somewhat of an upbeat and uplifting person, even under the circumstances, so I was taken aback by this sudden change. "Is Officer Locke there? I tried his cell phone, but it went to voice mail."

"Um . . . sure, h-hold on," I stammered, looking at Noah and motioning for him to come over. I mouthed *Chase* to him and he nodded.

"Hello?" he whispered, not wanting the girls to hear him. "Uh-huh . . . okay . . . I'll be there in"—he glanced at the clock on the wall—"half an hour." He hung up the phone and grabbed his keys off the counter.

"What's going on?" I asked, following him out the door. He seemed to be in a rush, and I couldn't tell if this was a good thing or a bad thing.

"I'll call you when I find out," he said, walking over to his car and unlocking the door.

I put my hand on the driver door to stop him from closing it. "What did he have to say? I know something is wrong, Noah, just tell me."

Noah took a deep breath and looked up at me. "Another girl's body was just found."

———

Chapter 8

Day Seventeen
—Lillian

Nearly four days had passed since I began working to loosen the bolts on my plaque, and *he* had only shown up twice. Both times he came downstairs, dropped off a bag of food, emptied our buckets and then left. He never said a word, never touched us, just dropped shit off and cleaned up. It made me both grateful and nervous—grateful that his time with us was so short, nervous that it was so robotic. I had a feeling that whoever he decided to abuse next was going to get it bad, but that was just a gut feeling.

At what I thought was the end of day four, I awoke to hear him shouting.

"Wake up, you stupid cow!"

His steps echoed through my small room along with the sound of the stairway door slamming open and shut. I stood up and looked around, making sure everything was in its place and no evidence of my hole in the corner or loosened bolts showed.

His keys jingled as he came up to my door and banged on it. "Your family's gonna cause you a world of hurt, little girl!" He opened my door. "Get over here."

I walked over to him until the chain pulled at my ankle, crossed my arms over my chest, and tried hard to look unfazed by his presence. He looked like a monster at the brink of insanity in front of me, his hair a mess, eyes wide with hatred, and I could tell he was clenching his teeth because his jaw muscles kept flinching.

"What do your parents do for a living?" he asked.

I stood there in confusion, my brow furrowing until it finally hit me.

Shit! My brother. He must be looking into this and trying to find me.

Not wanting to put Noah in any danger, I kept him out of my answer. "My mom is an art teacher in Eldorado Springs," I replied. "I don't know where my father is. Why, you want me to hook you up with some art lessons?"

He slapped me across the face. "Don't get smart with me, bitch! And you better not be lying or I'll make it so you'll be pushed around your precious track in a wheelchair for the rest of your life."

Track? How did he know I ran track?

My thoughts were ripped away from me when he slapped me across the face again.

"What, no witty remark? Don't have anything else you want to share with the class?"

I just stared at the floor, biting my lip, waiting for a metallic flavor to fill my taste buds, and willing myself to maintain control of my anger.

"Fine, if that's how you want to play it," he said, turning away from me and stalking out of the room, locking the door behind him.

The second I heard Anna cry out when he opened her door, I ran over to the wall and yelled, banging on it with my fists.

"Come on, Lilly," he laughed, and I heard him flip open his lighter. "I know this is your favorite part."

Anna screamed and I cried openly, resting my forehead against the wall. It was a double-edged sword talking shit now. Either I said something and he killed her, or I said something and he killed me. I banged my forehead against the wall, trying even harder to contain my anger.

"Fuck!" I yelled when I heard Anna scream again.

"Oh, please, is that the best you can do?" he moaned.

There was a loud bang against the wall, and it caused me to move away from it. He must have pushed Anna against it because his movements were causing the wall to bend.

"Please stop," Anna whimpered as the banging became more frequent.

I put my hands against the wall, laying my forehead back against it, trying to console Anna.

"Listen to my voice, Anna," I whispered. "I'm right here. Just pay attention to my voice." I felt my tears start to well up behind my eyes. "It'll all be over soon."

"It's not over till I say it's over, bitch," he yelled.

The wall thumped a few more times and then I heard Anna slump to the floor. He returned to my room, opening the door and barging in. He took me by the throat and shoved me against the wall.

"You're so heartless," he sneered, running his nose along my cheek. "To give them hope, raise their spirits." He pulled back and looked me straight in the eye. "I would say you torture them worse than me." He pulled his fist back and punched me straight in the stomach. He let me fall to the floor, where he proceeded to kick me in the side.

"God, it's such a turn on," he groaned. I rolled onto my back and bit my lip, holding my aching stomach. He reached down, picked me up, and threw me on the mattress. "Knowing that when I'm not here, you're here just making it worse for them," he smiled, lying on top of me and licking the side of my face. Trying to push him off me was useless. My body was in so much pain all I could do was close my eyes, hoping that this wouldn't last long.

He started rubbing himself against me, and I was unable to hold back the lone tear that escaped. I turned my head so he couldn't see it.

"God, you're beautiful," he whispered.

He continued rubbing himself against me while I just lay there, waiting for him to finish. He let out a low moan, his body trembling over me, then grabbed my face and plunged his tongue down my throat. He laughed when he was done, and stood up before walking toward my door.

"It may have taken me a little over two weeks, but I have yet to find a horse I couldn't break." He smiled with pride, shutting the door behind him.

I rolled over to my side and held myself. As soon as the main door was shut, Anna called out to me.

"Lee, are you okay?"

"Yeah."

"Forget about what he said, Lee. It's all bullshit," Linda called out.

I knew what she said was right, but I couldn't help but feel that, because of my mouth, some of their blood was on my hands. Too exhausted to answer, I just closed my eyes, letting sleep take over.

—◦◦◦—

Seventeen Days Missing
—Richard

"They all check out," Luke said, tossing his list on the kitchen table.

"I still have a weird feeling about this guy." Adam pushed the paper forward, pointing out one of the names at the bottom of the list.

"Just because the guy is an emo loner doesn't make him a serial kidnapper." Luke laughed. "I mean, that was Richard for years, and look at him. Maybe this guy just needs to get laid like Richie-boy did."

"Fuck off, Luke," I snapped.

"Okay, okay, sorry . . . bad joke," he apologized, setting down his beer. "Look, I'm just saying that this Thomas guy lives in a double wide in the middle of nowhere. Not a place to keep six girls."

"Five."

Four days earlier, the body of Ruth-Ann Summers had been found by the side of the road near Sugarloaf Mountain. Sugarloaf was forty-five minutes from Gold Hill where Nina Rosado was found, also by the side of the road. Just like Nina, Noah said Ruth's face was beaten to the point of being unrecognizable and both of her hands were missing. She had also been raped and starved. The worst thing was that she was found to be pregnant. That information alone almost killed me. Noah was damn near inconsolable. He and I knew these details and kept them to ourselves, not wanting to upset the others.

Sleep was becoming more and more difficult for me. Every night I would hear the echo of Lee's voice, screaming out in pain while being attacked by a man I couldn't see. I was surrounded by darkness, and no matter what direction I ran, I was never getting any closer to the source. Emma would even come wake me up when she heard me yelling Lee's name, now that I had moved in and was living on their couch.

"But look where he lives," Adam argued, pulling me out of my thoughts. "Gold Hill is here." He pointed on our little map. "And Sugarloaf is over there. They're small towns, just like Nederland. Nederland is a secluded area, and when I drove by the place you wouldn't have even noticed his home unless you were looking for it."

"Wait, you drove by it?" I asked, annoyed.

"Well, it had a gate around it. I couldn't drive up," he said. "I could see his trailer and that was about it. No other cars, buildings, or even a dog house nearby."

"Then I think we should at least tell Noah about this," Luke said, draining his beer.

"I agree," I answered, picking up the papers and following Luke toward the door. "If we leave now, we can make it to his place before traffic gets bad."

"I'll stay with the girls," Adam whispered, standing and facing us.

I walked over and gave him a hug. "You're a great friend, Adam. Thank you for your help."

He nodded and patted my back. "Anytime, bro. Now hurry up." He smiled, pushing me out the door.

—⁓⁓—

Chapter 9

Day Twenty
—Lillian

There was an eerie silence among us, besides the stupid record playing upstairs. I was about to say something when Anna started to sing.

Anna found comfort in singing after being brutalized. She was in too much pain to crawl off her mattress to our hole, where we would hold hands after he would hurt one of us. So she just lay on her mattress singing to us. Most of the time we joined her, needing to hear something other than the music that was on constant replay.

Each girl had found her own way to deal with the aftermath that was "The Douchebag". Linda would talk, sometimes for hours, but of course we never complained. Sara sought comfort in Anna. Their hole was about the same size as ours, so they were also able to hold hands. Kandace, being Kandace, found comfort in denting her walls with her fists. I couldn't blame her; I had, on occasion, done the same thing a few times. Some of my knuckles were still swollen.

I, on the other hand, had found a new hobby—our escape. Using the bobby pins Anna had given me, I had begun scraping off the rust around the bolts holding the plaque up against the wall. Satisfied that one of them looked good enough to try, I brought the bobby pins together sideways, placing them inside the crevice of the bolt. Like a makeshift flat-head screwdriver, I proceeded to try turning the bolt loose. The bobby pins kept cutting through my skin, causing me to bleed, but after a while the bolt turned. My heart stopped when I brought my fingers to it, unscrewing it the rest of the way. I looked at the bolt in my hand as if it were the best fucking thing I'd ever seen.

"Well, fuck me," I whispered, smiling to myself. "Broken horse, my ass."

As the hours passed, I quietly interacted with the girls as if nothing had changed. I continued working on loosening the other bolts, but listened as Anna and Linda began a debate over who had the sexier voice—George Clooney or Gerard Butler.

"What do you think, Lee?" Kandace asked, trying to pull me into the conversation.

"Sorry, girls, I'm not in this one."

"Traitor," Anna grumbled.

As fun as it seemed, I had more important things to take care of. With two bolts now loose, I was working on number three. For the last few days Anna had been asking me what I was doing, but I didn't have the heart to tell them. Not even Anna. I didn't know if this was going to work, and after what *he* had said, I didn't want to give them hope that it might.

"You lying bitch," he screamed upstairs.

I knew he was talking about me. I hid the bobby pins and screwed the bolts into the wall, leaving them loose. We were all silent as he ran down the stairs—not even bothering to turn off the music—and unlocked the door. I stood up and readied myself for the beating I knew for sure was coming. He unlocked my door and it flew open.

"My mother's an art teacher," he said in a mocking tone, walking in and slapping me across the face. I fell to the floor and covered my face as he continued to slap me. "I don't have a father." *Slap.* "But what about your brother, Lilly?" *Slap.* "Your brother, the cop!" *Slap.* "Walking around my town asking questions!" he screamed, slapping me one more time.

I tried to put my hands up to block the strikes, but he just pushed them away, hitting me harder. He picked me up and threw me at the wall. I bounced off it and landed on the floor with a thud. I heard him start to unbuckle his belt as he walked toward me. Everything was happening so fast that I had no time to protect myself, or even acknowledge the pain, before he was coming at me again.

"You have no respect, Lilly," he growled, wrapping his belt around his fist. "But trust me when I say that today you will learn never to lie to me again." He took me by my hair and proceeded to hit me so hard my vision blurred and my ears rang.

I woke up feeling a pressure on my chest. I was so dizzy that when I tried to lift my arms to push it away, they fell back down beside me. The more I started coming to, the more I realized my surroundings. My shirt was torn and my legs were bare except for one calf, which was tangled inside my jeans. The smell of sweat, blood, and stale cigarettes hung in the air, and a low moaning sounded in my ears. But the most horrifying thing of all was that *he* was still here, and he was on top of me.

Dear God, help me, he's inside me.

"No." The word sounded slurred as I tried my best to move. He just laughed and continued doing his business. "Nooo . . ." I whispered this time, tears welling up in my eyes.

He moaned. "Oh, yeah. Cry for me."

I don't know what it was about what he said, but it seemed to revive me. With all the strength I could muster, I reached up and scratched him, dragging my dirty nails deep and long across his cheek. He yelled, looking down at me with intense hatred in his eyes. He reached behind his body, and out of the corner of my eye I saw something shiny. Before I had a chance to react, he pressed the knife to my cheek and sliced it open.

"Now we match, whore."

With the blade pressed to my throat, causing me to go completely still, I didn't dare to do more than breathe and just lay there, letting him have his way with me. Within minutes—which felt like hours—he was done, moaning and grunting before resting his weight on me as if we were lovers.

"Not bad, Lilly," he said then kissed my uncut cheek. "Not bad at all."

He got up and moved off to the side, zipping up his pants and brushing himself off. "Here's a little something to think about while you're down here." I refused to acknowledge him while he walked over to the door. "If your brother, or one of his asshole friends, questions anyone about me again, they're dead."

I looked over at the door in horror as it slammed shut.

I wrapped my arms around my ever-thinning body, attempting to grasp some sense of the person that used to be there. The person with a life outside these hollow walls, the person with other people besides the four women who shared similar cells. The person who loved. A person, I hoped, who wasn't lost forever.

After telling the girls I wanted to be left alone, we all sat in silence. I couldn't bring myself to care if I hurt their feelings or not. I'm sure I wasn't alone when thinking how uncharacteristic it was for him to be playing that irritating song while he was down here with us, but for once I welcomed the noise that disguised my soft tears. Curled in a ball, still facing the door, I promised myself something I was afraid I wouldn't be able to keep.

Never again.

Never again would he touch me, and I was prepared to do anything to make sure I kept that promise to myself.

Twenty Days Missing
—Richard

Twenty days. Almost three weeks. Four hundred and eighty-some hours. Twenty-eight thousand, eight hundred plus minutes . . . I couldn't even think about how many seconds. Each one was just another reminder that Lee was still gone, still not in my arms, still suffering God knows what. My heart felt so hollow, but yet so heavy every time the phone rang. It was all in vain. That phone never had the voice I needed to hear.

Thomas Reed checked out. After telling Noah our idea, he agreed that it was something to look into. He talked to Agent Chase and they both went to Thomas Reed's home to question him. He explained that he shared a home with his brother, David, who worked long hours as a security guard up at one of the abandoned mines. He explained that David offered to house him because he was rarely home, and it made his brother feel better knowing there was someone watching over the place. Noah said that, from the looks of it, he seemed to be telling the truth. The trailer home was small and, although the property it sat on was large, all they found was a small shed behind the house that held tools. I guess Adam didn't see that during his little drive-by.

Noah and Agent Chase even went around town asking a few questions about Thomas Reed, and everyone said that he was quiet and shy, but a very polite young man. Even the local police said they'd never had any issues with the Reed brothers.

I felt defeated hearing that. I was convinced that this Thomas kid had to be our guy; it all seemed to fit. My head was telling me to trust Noah's words, but my heart couldn't. There was something about him. I couldn't explain, but I knew he had to know something.

Luke, Adam, and I took shifts watching him. We followed him around everywhere, when he was working, grocery shopping, or going to the drive-thru. I wanted eyes on him twenty-four seven. Luke and Adam tried their best to show interest in the guy, but I knew they felt the same way Noah did. I stopped asking them to follow Thomas after the third day. I didn't deny that I had become obsessed with watching him, but I refused to give up. He knew something, and I would be there to catch him when he slipped up.

"When was the last time you ate?" Emma asked. I had Thomas' schedule memorized by this point. I was never at the apartment, and when I was, it was always very late at night when I knew Thomas was asleep. I would drive home to shower, change, and head back, hoping to get a few hours' sleep before the sun rose. I would always park my car down the road, along the street, as the high brush camouflaged my car.

"I got a coffee and a muffin at the campus cart this morning," I said. I typically didn't answer my phone when I was watching Thomas, but he was eating lunch at the moment, so I was outside smoking. Seeing it was Emma, I answered because I thought maybe she might have heard something new about Lee, which wasn't the case.

"Richard, where are you? I'm sending Adam over there to switch places with you." She sighed. "You need to eat and get some sleep."

"Don't, Emma, I'm fine." I stopped paying attention to Emma when I noticed Thomas get up from his chair and throw his trash away. "I gotta go, Emma. Talk to you later." I hung up the phone, not caring what she was about to say. It wasn't that I didn't trust Adam or Luke—I knew they would help if I asked. I just didn't trust that they believed me when I said this *was* the guy.

I maintained my distance, as always, trying to seem inconspicuous while continuing to follow him. Thomas went through his normal routine at work. He assisted the coaches with paperwork, set the fields up, and helped put equipment away. I stood behind the bleachers, as always, adding to the ever growing pile of cigarette butts accumulating at my feet. I choked on the one I was smoking when Adam came up behind me.

"Dude, seriously?" He laughed, looking down at the mess at my feet. "I hope those weren't your so-called coffee and muffin this morning."

"No," I replied, stubbing out my cigarette and turning my attention back to Thomas.

"Why don't you let me take over for a while, Richard?" Adam said, patting my back and glancing over at the field. "Go take a shower and get some good food in your system."

"I'm fine, Adam. I'll come home later on tonight and eat."

"When? At two in the morning?" he snapped. "Just so you can get back here by four after *maybe* two hours of sleep?"

I was taken aback for a second by his sudden change in attitude, but masked it and turned my attention back to Thomas. "This isn't a debate, Adam."

"No, it's more like an intervention."

I was growing annoyed. I'd already had a similar encounter with Luke about this, and I wasn't about to deal with it again. "I understand you're all worried, but I don't have time for this. It's been twenty days, Adam—"

"You think we don't know that?" he bellowed, pushing me against one of the metal pillars. "You think you're the only one that misses her? She has a mom and brother at her apartment that are in agonizing pain." He slammed his hand against his chest. "Friends who are worried that they will never get the chance to tell her how wonderful she is." He pushed me again, forcing me to look at him. "A best friend, *your* sister, *my* girlfriend, who cries herself to sleep *every night* because she feels that she didn't just lose a sister, but a brother as well."

I couldn't help but let a few tears fall. Adam was right. I had pushed everyone away in my need to find some form of solace with Lee being gone. Adam pulled me into a hug and allowed me to cry. "All we're asking for is a few hours."

"How many?" I asked, trying to steady my breathing.

"Eight hours."

I pulled away, shaking my head. "That's too long," I argued.

"For us, or for you?" he asked.

For me. "For you."

"Look, I'll take the first four and Luke will take the last. You can relieve him from watch at"—he looked down at his phone —"two in the morning. It gives you enough time to eat, shower, and get a few hours of sleep."

I sighed and caved. He was right, again, but he knew that. Adam had always been the voice of reason in any situation. And when we did find Lee, I didn't want her coming home to a mess of a boyfriend. "Thanks, Adam. You know—for everything." I smiled.

"Yeah, yeah." He chuckled. "Go home and get some rest. I'll have my phone on if anyone needs to reach me."

I walked to my car feeling anxious. This would be the first time in days that I'd have to confront the realization of what was going on back at the apartment. The darkness that seemed to consume that place was haunting. It was as if Lee was the light, and with her gone we were blind, surrounded by constant darkness. My motivation to keep going was to find Lee, and to find the monster who took her. I turned around and looked at Thomas one last time.

I swear to God if you have my girl, I will make you pay.

—∿∿—

Chapter 10

Day Twenty-Three
—Lillian

He hadn't come down in a few days again. I found it comforting that he wasn't around, but a few of the girls were getting scared that we would end up starving to death.

"We would die of dehydration first," Sara said.

"Thanks a lot, Sara," Kandace yelled. "I appreciate the biology session. Now shut the fuck up."

I hadn't talked much since the attack. I would talk to Anna a little bit, but that was it. As much as I knew that the other girls understood how I felt, their words fell on my ears like faint whispers. My mind wasn't there. It never was. My mind was on Ruth and Nina. I could feel it in my bones that I was next. It was just a matter of time.

I had been able to get three out of the four bolts loose, but number four was being a bitch. My hands ached from the bobby pins cutting into them. It also didn't help that it was getting colder and I was always shivering. My tattered shirt had been useless to keep me warm, so I ripped it into strips and wrapped them around my hands to stop the bleeding. I tried everything to get that fucking plaque off, but even with just the one bolt holding it in place, it held on to the wall like a champ.

Fatigue was also starting to become a problem. Due to the lack of food and water, it was harder to keep up my strength.

"Can I just state the obvious for a minute?" Anna grumbled. "I'm fucking starving."

"You think something happened to him?" Linda asked.

"You mean like maybe he got caught?" I answered, pulling at the plaque again. "I doubt it."

"Why do you say that?" Linda replied. "And what are you doing over there?"

I sighed, walking away from the loose plaque, stretching my arms. "If he was stupid enough to get caught, he would have been arrested a while ago."

"Okay, I'll buy that Lee, but what *are* you doing?" Linda asked again.

I didn't want to say anything, but I knew I had to tell them sooner rather than later. "Girls, I have something to tell you, but I don't want you to get excited. Not yet, anyway."

"What's going on?" Anna asked.

"You know that plaque on the wall, the one holding our chains?"

"Yeah?" four voices replied.

"Well, I've been getting the bolts loose off of mine."

"What?" Kandace yelled. "How the fuck did you do that?"

"Well, Anna gave me some bobby pins a while ago, and I've been using them to loosen the bolts on the plaque."

There was an unnerving silence among them that seemed to last a lifetime.

"What are you going to do if you get loose?" Sara asked, breaking the silence.

"Bash his fucking head in, I hope," Anna hollered. We all kind of laughed at that.

"To be honest, I haven't thought about it." I sighed. "Right now plan A is to just get this fucking chain off the wall. Plan B I'll figure out once I get there."

"You're going to get yourself killed, Lee," Kandace snapped. "When he comes down here and sees what you've done, he's gonna kill you just like Nina and Ruth."

"He has to show up first," I grumbled.

"Have you thought about what this means for the rest of us?" Kandace asked. "He might think we can all do it—that we're all in on it. He'll end up killing us all."

I never thought about it that way. Maybe I was being selfish. I had to be honest with myself; I was thinking about getting myself out of this room.

Before, it was about getting all of us out, but when he threatened my family, my motives shifted. It was about getting out and helping them. There was no way to change what I had already done, but I had to fix it.

"I won't let him, Kandace. I swear."

"Oh, really?" she scoffed. "And how do you plan to do that?"

"Because if I get this plaque off, and he's in the room with me, he's not coming out."

"Lee, just please be careful," Anna whispered. I looked down at our little hole, walked over to it, and stuck my hand through. She must have seen my hand because she took it.

"I will, Anna," I promised, gripping her hand. "I'm gonna get out of this room, and the first door I'm breaking down is yours." I kept my voice low, not wanting the others to hear me.

"Can I say something and not sound like a sap?" she said with a slight sniffle.

I couldn't help but smile at her question. "Sure, what is it?"

"Even though I have never seen you, I feel like you're a sister in a way. Like we're some twisted, fucked-up family down here. I just want you to know, if I don't make it, that I love you."

"I love you, too, Anna," I whispered.

I wasn't just saying that to make her feel better, I had honest love for her. I loved all of them, but there was little comfort coming from such a truth. The last annoying bolt in the wall was causing some serious problems with my confidence. It was as if it was mocking me. No matter how hard I pulled, tugged, and bled, it wouldn't budge. After the first bolt had popped off, the others seemed to come off like a breeze, but not that one.

I felt Anna's hand become loose in mine and I realized she had fallen asleep. I stood up and stretched. My body was still recovering from the latest attack, and I was more than confident that if I were to look in a mirror I wouldn't even be able to recognize myself. My right eye was still swollen, and looking down I could tell that one of my ribs was fractured.

Time was running out for us. I could feel it. It was as if there were a giant guillotine blade over my neck, just waiting to fall.

———

The sound of footsteps coming down the stairs woke me. I rushed over to the plaque on the wall and screwed the bolts back in place. I'd be damned if I was going to get caught now. A few locks turned and the door squeaked open, and then shut. I felt myself tensing up, but that receded when a voice spoke.

"Everyone turn around and face the wall, your back facing the door."

It wasn't *him*. It was someone different. This man's voice was softer. His footsteps were softer, too, I realized. But I did as I was told and stood in front of the wall, my back to the door.

One by one I heard the doors opening and then shutting, with nothing being said. No crying, screaming, or whimpering. Finally, he came to my door. It opened, and I heard a small hiss escape his mouth. I wrinkled my nose at the faint smell of cheap cologne, but then there was also something else. Something familiar that I couldn't seem to place. My door shut, and he left just as fast as he had arrived. I turned around to see a bag of food, two bottles of water, and a small pile of clothes left just within my reach.

"Anna?" I called out.

"Yeah?"

"Are you looking at what I'm looking at?"

"Uh-huh."

"Who was that, you guys?" I asked, walking over and gathering the food, water, and clothing, and taking it back over to the mattress.

"I don't know," Kandace replied. "That was the first time I've ever heard this guy."

I didn't know if I should be nervous or not. There were now two of these assholes up there.

—◦◦◦—

Twenty-Three Days Missing
—Richard

Thomas hadn't left his house in three days. After Luke went to the university and asked, in a very nonchalant way, where he was, he found out that Thomas had called in sick with the flu. I didn't buy it for a second.

Noah was back in town, so I asked Luke to take over watch while I talked to Noah. Adam called to say that he was going to take the women grocery shopping, and I was glad that Noah and I would be alone. When I reached the apartment, I found him out on the patio, smoking. I whipped out a cigarette and stood next to him.

"Heard anything?" I asked, lighting my smoke.

"Nothing you want to hear," he grumbled. Noah agreed that Thomas was someone to keep tabs on, but not in the way I was doing it.

"Seriously, isn't there any news?" I pushed.

He shook his head. "No, bro, I'm sorry."

A minute later Lee and Emma's home phone rang, and Noah flicked out his cigarette and jogged over to answer it. I stood there staring out at the scenery, thinking of nothing else but my beautiful girl. Anytime I got tired, or found myself not paying attention, I would dial Lee's cell phone, just to hear the sound of her voice on the voice mail greeting. In the beginning, I needed to be alone when I called her cell. I wanted to be able to cry without having to worry about people seeing, but now it didn't matter. Hearing her voice was my wake-up call. Her voice would pulsate through me like a shot of caffeine.

"No . . . no, thank you," Noah said, writing something down on a nearby notepad. He hung up the phone, and then took his cell out of his pocket, dialed a number, and started talking. I couldn't tell what he was saying, but when he saw me watching him he hung up the phone, ripped off the piece of paper, and grabbed his coat. "I gotta run."

"What's going on?" I asked. I found myself asking him that a lot lately, and it was starting to piss me off. I was tired of playing catch-up to Noah's constant phone calls.

"Just something I have to verify. Keep your cell on you," he said in a rush as he ran out the door.

I stood there in a daze, wondering what the hell just happened. I went over to the notepad, picked it up, and took it into the kitchen. I turned the stove light on and held the paper below it, hoping to make out what he had written. The one thing I could make out was the name David.

Who the hell was David?

Chapter 11

Day Twenty-Five
—*Lillian*

I woke up crying again. I had been dreaming of Richard a lot, and it seemed that every time I did I'd wake up thinking that he was next to me. I would reach over, assuming I would feel him, but there was nothing there. There was never anything but the cold, dirty mattress that lay beneath me. Some nights I knew that I was dreaming. It was always the same dream: we were lying in bed, facing each other, and we would just stare at one another. When I would start to wake up, I would watch him fade away, and I would just cry. I wanted to reach out for him, to yell out his name, but I never did. I knew there was no point. I curled myself around the large flannel shirt that was given to me by the guy we now called 'Number Two', and bit my lip to hush my tears.

Number Two seemed nice. He never once hurt us or yelled, but came down every day to bring us food and empty our buckets. I didn't know what to make of it. We were never allowed to look at him, or even speak, but there was just something about him—something familiar.

I was pulled out of my thoughts by the sound of footsteps above us. They were loud and heavy, and I knew it was *him*. He was back.

"Wake up," I yelled, pounding on the wall. "He's back."

Before anyone had the chance to say anything, the soft voice of Patsy

Cline that had filtered through the air nonstop for days was cut off. I looked over at the plaque against the wall and gave that last bolt the evil eye as I heard his footsteps come down the stairs. I stood up when I heard the jingle of the keys unlocking the door. When he opened the heavy metal door that led to our hallway of cells, I almost had to cover my ears with how bad the echo of the hinges squeaked, and I couldn't help but jump when he slammed it behind him. He didn't make a sound, which made me anxious because he always had some stupid quip to throw at us.

He walked down the hall, and opened one of the other girl's doors before closing it behind him. If he spoke anything, it must have been in a whisper, but I knew he was with one of the girls when I heard a chain clang against the floor. Normally I welcomed some form of silence against the screams and cries, having to cover my ears and hum just to block it out, but this was different. I'd never heard such silence down here, and it scared the shit out of me.

A sharp gasp sliced through the air, followed by a grunt, and then nothing. What also scared me was how quick he was. I could guess how long he had been in the cell, but compared to his other visits, there was no way he had come down here for his normal business.

I didn't realize I was holding my breath until the door slammed open again. I couldn't help the shudder of breath that escaped my throat when I heard something being dragged across the floor. I fell to my knees and wrapped my arms around my bruised body, letting warm tears fall from my eyes as thump after thump after thump echoed up the stairwell.

It was the sound of a head hitting the stairs. He had murdered another girl.

My body shook with rage when I heard his footsteps on the stairs again before he shut the main door and locked it. I was breathing heavily by that point and almost screamed when Kandace's shaky voice spoke out.

"It was Linda."

"She didn't do anything!" Sara yelled. "She never fought back or cried. She was his favorite."

It was true. Linda, out of all of us, was treated better in the sense that he didn't beat or torture her the way he did us.

"He's going to kill us all," Sara said, on the verge of hysteria. "We're not gonna make it out. We're not gonna make it out. We're not gonna make it out."

"Will you just shut up, for fuck's sake?" Kandace screamed. "We don't need you to state the obvious."

But there was no use trying to calm Sara. It was as if her spirit, and sanity, had been broken. I couldn't blame her; if I wasn't so angry I'd be a wreck, too, but I didn't have time to let my sadness take over. I had to get that damn bolt off. I used my newfound anger as my strength and motivation while I pulled against my chain. With the three freed bolts kept in my pocket, I lifted my foot up against the wall and, with all the strength I could muster, started to pull. Visions of Ruth's face and Linda's voice played over and over as I tightened my sore hand around the chain. I tried to maintain my focus on the job at hand, but my mind wandered to the night Richard and I began dating.

I took a sip of my drink and bobbed my head to the music. Gavin from the track team stood next to me, but for the life of me I had no idea why I had agreed to go out with him. He was such a freak, and not in a good way. The only reason I had agreed to the date was because I knew Richard would be at the party, and I wanted to make him jealous. I'd grown so sick and tired of the awkward tension between the two of us that I had now stooped to belittling myself into accepting dates from mouth breathers.

"Hey, Lee, why don't we get out of here? Don't you think it's a little loud?" Gavin asked, plugging his ears and leaning toward me.

"Um, no thanks." I smiled. "I'm good."

"Well, how about we go outside? Just to get a little air?" he suggested.

I thought about it for a second and decided that I could handle that.

I hadn't realized how smoky it was in there until we stepped out onto the front porch. It was slightly chilly outside, and I crossed my arms over my bare shoulders to keep them warm. Why, oh why, did I have to wear a halter top in September?

"Isn't that a little better?" Gavin asked. "Now I can hear what you're saying."

'Yeah, as if you even give a shit. You were looking at my boobs the whole time. You're still looking at my boobs,' I thought. In reality, I had been ready to end the date the second I got out of the car. I hadn't seen Richard all night, and my ass and I were growing incredibly annoyed with Gavin's wandering hands.

"Yeah, I guess," was all I could muster.

For the next hour, all I could do was smile and nod occasionally as Gavin blabbered on about politics and philosophy. I excused the yawn that I couldn't hold back, explaining that I had gotten up early that morning for track practice. I'd be lying if I said I wasn't relieved when he asked if I wanted to go home. All I wanted to do was take a hot shower and dive into a pint of Cherry Garcia ice cream.

When we got back to my place, Gavin walked me to my apartment. I repeatedly assured him it wasn't necessary, but still found us both in front of my door anyway. I unlocked it and put on the fakest smile possible. "I had a nice time, Gavin. Thank you for inviting me to the party."

"Me, too, Lee." He smiled, rubbing the back of his neck with his hand. "Maybe we can go see a movie or something?"

Oh crap. "Maybe." I smiled, giving a small nod. "Well good night, Gavin." I turned to go in but was stopped when he took my wrist in his hand.

"Lee, I was wondering . . . I mean, what I wanted to ask was . . ." I kept looking down at his hand on my wrist as he stuttered with his words. "Would it be okay if . . ."

"Gavin, let go of my wrist," I asked nicely.

"It's just that I really like you and . . ."

"Let go of my wrist," I said firmly, feeling a little nervous.

"I was thinking maybe you might want . . ."

What the fuck was this guy's problem? I couldn't even comprehend anything that he was saying because all I knew was that his grip, for some reason, was becoming tighter around my wrist. My heart started to pound in my chest, and my stomach started to feel heavy.

"Gavin, let go of my damn wrist," I yelled.

"What?" he asked, looking surprised by my outburst.

Suddenly Gavin was pulled away from me and thrown to the ground. "The lady said to let go," Richard growled. He went at Gavin in two strides and picked him up by his collar. "And when a lady says let go, you fucking let go. Got that, bro?" he yelled, causing Gavin to shiver and nod in agreement. "If I see you so much as look at her the wrong way, I will break your neck. Understand?" Gavin just nodded again and ran for his car when Richard let him go.

I stood there in shock, holding my wrist to my chest with my other hand. It would bruise, but I'd be fine. Richard stood there for a long time; his breathing was labored, and he looked as stiff as a board. It took a few tries, but by the third time I called his name he finally turned and looked at me. He saw me holding my wrist and immediately came to my side to look at it.

"We should put ice on that," he whispered.

Richard waited on the patio while I washed my face and changed. I wanted to shower, but I didn't want to keep him waiting. Normally I would have reveled in the chance to wear something a little . . . smaller, but for some reason I felt the need to cover up. So I put on a pair of loose-fitting pajamas and followed the familiar smell of smoke that led outside.

"Hey." I smiled, running my fingers through my wet hair.

"How's your wrist?" he asked, flicking his cigarette to the ground.

I lifted my ice-packed wrist, which Richard had taped, and sighed. "Sore, but I'll live."

"Promise me you'll never go out with him again, Lee," he muttered, taking my wrist gently into his hands and checking the tape again.

"I won't," I whispered back.

There was an awkward silence between us again, an awkwardness I unfortunately had grown accustomed to, but thankfully he spoke. "Why did you?"

"Why did I what?"

He sighed, taking a step back from me, and ran his hand through his hair. "Why did you even go out with that guy?"

"Well, it's not like I have guys breaking down my door, Richard." I chuckled. "It felt nice to be wanted for once."

"Is that how you feel? Like you're not wanted?"

I shifted my weight from one foot to the other. I bit my lip and looked down, nodding slowly. I felt him move toward me and I couldn't help but feel my heart start to race.

"Lee, I . . ."

I looked up at him and saw it in his eyes. He wanted me; I knew it. His need for me radiated off his body like electricity. He raised his right hand slowly toward my face, and I closed my eyes in preparation for the feeling I was about to experience. A feeling I'd been waiting for far too long.

"I have to go."

By the time I opened my eyes, I was watching him as he gathered up his jacket and headed for the door. He wouldn't even look at me as he exited the apartment, shutting the door softly behind him. I just stood there dumbfounded. 'Why won't he kiss me? Was I wrong? Was I reading signs that weren't there?' I wondered to myself.

I went over and sat at the small patio table, letting my head rest on top of my arms. I couldn't help the tears that seeped from my eyes as I cried at my idiocy. I cried because I felt stupid, I cried because I felt lonely, and I cried because at that moment I gave up on ever having Richard Haines.

"Lee?"

My heart stopped when I heard him whisper my name. I slowly turned to see Richard standing behind me looking just as pained as I felt. He let his jacket fall to the ground and took my face in his warm hands. He wiped my tears away with his thumbs and leaned his forehead against mine. "I want you," he whispered, pressing his soft lips against mine.

"Lee!"

I was pulled away from my thoughts when Anna yelled my name.

"I'm here. Sorry, I just kinda spaced out for a minute." I grunted, continuing to pull at my chain.

"Okay," she simply answered.

Thinking of Richard calmed me down, but at the same time pissed me off. I needed that anger, that extra boost of energy that seemed to fuel my fire. "God fucking dammit!" I screamed, slamming my chain on the floor.

"Still no luck?" Kandace asked.

"No, I just like taking the Lord's name in vain for the hell of it," I said, leaning against the wall and sliding down. I pulled my knees to my chest and wrapped my arms around them. I needed to focus on something, anything but the dull, aching pain in my chest. I was letting my mind wander on too many things, and all it was doing was causing me to become overwhelmed.

When kids at school were overwhelmed with exams or projects, they mostly drank to calm down and then crammed at the last minute. That had never worked for me. Running had always been my go-to for decompressing. So I decided to focus on running. I closed my eyes and rested my forehead on my knees. I could almost hear my feet pounding against the ground, feel my ponytail swishing back and forth, and the steady rush of wind blowing past me. This was my safe zone, my sanctuary.

"I'll make it so you'll be pushed around your precious track in a wheelchair for the rest of your life."

For some reason those words echoed through my head like a high-pitched scream, but with this scream came a realization.

He knows me.

It was starting to make sense now.

"Anna, do you play any sports?"

"I play softball."

"At school?"

"Yeah, why?"

I stood up and started pacing.

"Kandace, what about you?" I yelled.

"Soccer," she replied in awe. "And you run track. That son of a bitch." I was grateful that Kandace was catching on. "Sara, what sport do you play?"

"Lacrosse," she whispered.

"Linda and Nina must have played sports, too," I said, mainly to myself, but knew the other girls heard me.

"So you think he's someone that works at the school? Maybe in the athletic department?" Anna asked.

"No, not him, but I think Number Two does," I concluded.

"Why do you think it's him?" Sara asked.

"Because every time he comes down here, I smell something familiar about him. Something I couldn't place until just now." I smiled, feeling relieved that I had finally found a main piece of the puzzle. "He smells like . . ."

"Chalk," the four of us said simultaneously.

"Holy shit, I know him," Kandace yelled excitedly. "He chalks the practice field every morning. I used to see him all the time. Connie, our captain, kinda had a thing for him. Damn, what is his name?"

At that moment, I couldn't care less what Number Two's name was. I wanted to know *his* name. That was going to be my card to get him in here when I got that final bolt loose. My previous assumption of him killing me off next was wrong, but it made me realize that if he was going to start killing us off one by one, he was probably going to leave me for last.

Twenty-Five Days Missing
—Richard

"Who the fuck is David?" Adam asked.

"There isn't one David on the list." Luke sighed, tossing the sheet across the table.

After Noah left the other night, I started focusing my attention on him and not Thomas. Noah seemed to be on a different track than the rest of us, spending more and more time around Agent Chase and the police station, and I couldn't help but be annoyed at his secretiveness. I called Chase and asked him if there were any leads, but he just said they were doing the best that they could, and that he would call if anything came up. I knew I was being blown off, so I concluded that I had to keep doing this on my own.

"Well, we have to figure this out. We're running out of time," I said firmly, taking a drink of my beer.

Luke let out a long breath and leaned back in his chair. "Maybe if we just *asked* Noah—"

"No." I cut him off quietly, not wanting to upset the women in the other room. "Noah and Agent Chase are no longer an option. They are hiding something from us, and I'm not going to listen to another speech about being called when something is found."

"So does this mean we're no longer stalking Tom?" Adam asked.

"For now," I nodded. "Now we're following Noah."

"Have you lost your fucking mind?" Luke yelled.

"Shh," Adam and I whispered, pointing toward the other room.

Luke motioned his head toward the front door, and we all got up and shuffled out. I lit a cigarette the second the door shut.

"Dude, are you seriously asking us to stake out Lee's brother?" Luke groaned in annoyance.

"I'm not asking you to do shit," I fired back. "You wanted to help, and I really appreciate that, but I'm focusing my attention on Noah for a while. If you want to join, then the more the merrier, but I know Noah is hiding something about all of this and I'm not going to be satisfied until I find out what the hell it is."

"And you think it has something to do with a guy named David?" Adam mumbled to himself, lifting the piece of paper that had the imprint of Noah's message on it. He held it up toward the sun, trying to make it out better. "Can I take this? I know a guy in the science department who might be able to help."

"Sure. Do whatever you can." I nodded.

Luke and I stood there as we watched Adam drive away.

"I'm not saying I won't help, Richard. I'm just saying I don't like it." My brother sighed, crossing his arms.

"Neither do I, bro, but I don't see any other choice."

We both stopped talking when the front door opened and Sadie stepped out. "Hey, did Emma leave with Adam?"

"No. I thought she was in there with you guys?" I asked, confused.

"Well, she went to lie down, but when I checked on her she wasn't in her room," Sadie said hesitantly.

Luke and I ran inside and went straight to Emma's room. The cold October wind swept through her open window, but what stood out was the fact that her screen had been taken off. Emma would never have done that. I ran over to the window and hopped out, grateful they lived on the first floor. I looked down at the ground and saw two large footprints facing the window, and right off to the side was Emma's cell phone. I picked it up and looked at Luke through the window.

Sadie came in and looked around at our faces. Not needing to be told, she collapsed on Emma's bed crying, holding herself as she rocked back and forth.

"Don't say it, Richard," Luke warned. "Don't you fucking say it."

"He got her," I gasped, holding onto the windowsill so I wouldn't fall over.

Luke came over, lifted me through the window, and threw me on the floor. He grabbed me and pulled me up, shaking me roughly. "Don't you fucking say it! Not Emma! Not my little Emma." He fell to his knees and wept as I just stood there. I couldn't feel anything. My whole body felt numb.

Not realizing Emma's phone was in my hand, I almost ignored the fact that it was vibrating. I looked at the phone and saw that it was Adam calling. When I opened the phone, I heard his voice, but couldn't find the words to answer.

"Hello? Hello, Emma?" Adam's voice rang out, but I couldn't answer. All I could do was hold my crying brother and pray.

―∽―

Chapter 12

Day Twenty-Six
—Lillian

I was sitting in silence, trying to force down yet another dry bologna sandwich, when the sound of doors slamming and loud footsteps echoed overhead. I quickly checked to make sure the bolts were back in the wall and my hole covered with the carpet in the corner. I sat back on my mattress and waited to see if it was either going to be *him* or Number Two. I closed my eyes and tried to concentrate on the sounds I heard.

There was more than one set of footsteps coming down the stairs, which meant both of them were here.

They were arguing with each other. *He* was saying things like, "This wasn't part of the plan" and "This better be worth it."

When they made it to the bottom of the stairs, I heard what I believed to be Ruth's old room being opened and the sound of chains being moved around. If they had gone to one of the other rooms, I would have heard the girls whimper or cry, but they were silent. They must have been listening as intently as I was.

My eyes snapped open when Ruth's door was slammed shut and the lock turned.

"Let's go. We'll come check on her in an hour." Our captor's voice sounded gritty and annoyed, letting Number Two know he didn't have the option to disagree.

We all waited for them to leave, and the music to turn back on, before any of us spoke.

Sara's voice echoed out first. "I guess we have a new roommate."

"Poor thing," Anna whispered. "I wonder who she is?"

I didn't answer, nor did anyone else. It didn't matter who she was, because somehow she'd ended up here with us. Anger boiled in me as I imagined that poor girl waking up in there, chained and confused, not knowing what happened or what would happen. What pissed me off even more was how quick he worked to add new girls to torture.

Needing to keep my mind off our newest arrival, I went back to chipping away at the bolt in the wall. I could hear Anna digging in the dirt next to me, and that was fine. It kept her from wanting to chat with me, and for some reason I just wasn't in the mood for it. I needed to focus on the task at hand.

After a while, a groggy voice rang out. "Hello?"

I was shocked by how familiar it sounded. And when she called out again, a feather could have knocked me over.

"Emma?" I said, my voice just barely over a whisper.

No, it couldn't be.

"Lee? Lillian . . . is that you?" she asked.

Oh my God.

I felt as if my heart had been ripped out of my chest. Fear and rage pumped through my body even as my brain spiraled in confusion.

Emma didn't play sports. She didn't have an athletic bone in her body. Why would he take Emma?

I stood and moved closer to the door, almost falling when the chain pulled at my ankle. "Emma, what are you doing here? How did you get here?" I asked, trying to keep my voice calm but failing.

"I don't . . . I don't know. All I remember is lying down to take a nap."

A nap? Holy shit. He had been inside our apartment, in her *room*. That thought alone made my body vibrate with outrage.

"Lee, I'm chained in here."

"Welcome to the club, sister," Kandace said, laughing bitterly. "We all are."

"Who said that?" Emma asked.

"My name is Kandace."

There was a pause before Emma said anything.

"Kandace Veccio, right?"

"Yeah, how did you know that?" Kandace asked.

"Are Anna Lin, Linda Baker and Sara Turner down here, too?"

When Emma said Linda's name, my eyes welled with tears.

"Not Linda. Linda was—" I had to stop and take a deep breath before I could keep going. "Linda didn't make it."

There was a moment of silence between all of us, but I couldn't stand it. I needed to know what was going on.

"Emma, are you okay?" I asked.

"Yeah, I'm okay."

Her voice sounded calm, which shocked me, but Emma was always better at hiding her emotions than I was. Where I lashed out, she calmed down. I yelled and she got quiet.

"I think I know this song," she said, humming along with the chorus.

"Yeah, well, get used to it," Kandace replied. "He plays it on repeat all day."

I started pacing inside my room, the cuff around my ankle cutting into my skin every time I reached my limit from one side to the other. To say I was confused was an understatement. So many questions were swirling around my head, I had to say them out loud in hopes that maybe one of the others could figure it out.

"I don't get it. Why did he take you?" I asked. "You don't play any sports."

"What do sports have to do with it?"

"The one thing we all have in common is that we all play sports," Kandace answered.

"Oh, well, yeah. Lee's right, I don't play sports," Emma said. "I just watch."

Maybe that's where he saw Emma? She did go to a few of my track meets during the season.

"Emma?" Anna called out. "What day is it?"

"October twenty-sixth, well, if it's not the twenty-seventh already."

"It's been twenty-six days?" I asked. "I thought it had been longer."

"Lee, I'm just so happy you're alive. You have no idea how hard your brother and Richard have been looking for you." Emma's voice trembled as I heard her sniffle to keep her tears away.

A smile swept over my face as tears spilled over with no shame. They were looking for me, they hadn't given up, and that alone gave me more incentive to keep fighting.

"What about the rest of us?" Sara asked.

"Yes, they are looking for all of you. It's been all over the news. Everyone is trying real hard."

"Not hard enough," Kandace whispered loud enough for all of us to hear.

Annoyed by her ungratefulness, I was about to yell at Kandace to shut up when the music was cut off and the sound of footsteps coming down the stairs stopped me. Rage and fear settled over me at the idea that he might be coming down here to hurt Emma. I needed to prepare myself to be ready to piss him off. To get him to want to come into my room instead of hers.

"Emma, listen to me, whatever happens, whatever you hear, don't scream," I said. "Promise me, Emma. Promise me that no matter what happens down here, or whatever happens to me, don't react. Swear it."

I never got Emma's answer, but I hoped in her heart she promised me. As the heavy door that led down to us opened, I stood up and planned in my head what I was going to say to get him in my room.

"You have ten minutes, and then you're done," he said. "Understand?"

"Yes," Number Two responded.

So he wasn't going in, but Number Two was? Number Two had only ever come to give us supplies and clean out our buckets. He unlocked Emma's door, and she gasped and let out a soft whimper.

"Very nice, very nice indeed," *he* said smugly. "You sure you don't want to share?"

I was ready to yell out right then and there, but Number Two's response beat me to the chase.

"She is mine."

"Fine," *he* said an annoyed tone. "Twenty minutes, and that's all."

I heard Emma's door shut and only one set of footsteps go back upstairs. Number Two must have been in there with her, and the thought made me sick to my stomach. I fell to my knees, my chain held tight within my grasp, as I strained to hear what was going on in the other room.

"Hello," I heard Number Two say.

Chains rattled and then they stopped.

"Does that hurt?" he asked.

Surprised by how genuine his voice sounded, I took a deep breath, trying to steady my rapid heart.

"Will you please sit with me? I swear I'll stay right here. Look . . . ." I heard some rustling, and what must have been him sitting on the floor. "I won't move, I promise."

There was a small pause before he spoke again. "I know you're not dumb, Emma," he whispered. "I know you know who I am. I could tell by the look on your face when I walked in."

My heart started beating loudly once again. I could feel a slight sheen of perspiration coat my body, and even a little bit of bile rose in my throat. *She knew him?* I was unsure if I should respond, but I decided that maybe it was for the best that I didn't.

"Thank you," Emma said.

"For what?" he asked.

"For not thinking I'm dumb."

I was still confused about why they took her. She didn't play sports, and hardly went to any of the games. The only time she did was when I ran. I had been so convinced that it was sports that connected all of us. Granted, I didn't know if Ruth or Nina played sports, but Emma was proof that my theory was null and void.

"Are you going to hurt me—like the others?" I heard Emma ask, her voice cracking a little at the end.

"No, that's . . . that's him. Not me."

"So you don't . . ."

"No!" I heard him shout, cutting off Emma. "No, I don't force . . . I mean . . . I wouldn't do that."

I'd give the prick that much, he hadn't laid one finger on any of us. Yet.

"Thomas—"

"Tom."

Thomas. His name was Thomas.

I mulled over that new bit of information, trying to see if I could remember anyone named Thomas, but I couldn't. How could Emma know this person when I didn't?

Emma and Thomas' voices became quiet after that. I would catch a word here and there, but I wasn't able to make out the conversation.

The minutes felt like hours while I sat there waiting for anything. Either their voices to pick up so I could hear them, or for *him* to come back down, or for Emma to cry out because Thomas was attacking her. But even if that happened, I was stuck and unable to do anything but sit and wait.

"You mean that, Emma?" Thomas said with excitement in his voice. "You'll stay with me forever?"

My eyes widened and I turned my ear toward the door.

Stay forever? What the hell?

"As long as you live up to your end, I'll stay," Emma answered.

"I swear, Emma. I swear on my life I won't let anything happen to them."

I heard Emma let out a squeak, like she had been startled, and that led me to stand up and stalk toward the door until the chain pulled against my ankle.

"You've made me so happy, Emma. I swear I'll earn your love."

"What the fuck is he talking about?" I whispered.

All talking stopped when the sound of footsteps came down the stairs. I took a few steps back out of instinct.

"Time's up," *he* yelled. "Are you decent?" He chuckled as he tapped on Emma's door.

"Yes," Tom answered.

I heard Emma's door open and bang against the wall. "How's the new girl?"

"It's not like that," Tom answered angrily.

"Still a fucking pussy, I see," *he* said in a very matter-of-fact way. "That's why you can't hold on to a woman. You need to learn to take charge. Maybe I should go in there and at least soften her up a little."

I heard Emma whimper and that caused me to finally take action. I'd be damned if that piece of shit was going to touch my best friend.

"Ha!" I called out.

I heard a growl and then *he* came over and banged on my door. "You shut the fuck up bitch or . . . you know what?" I heard him pull out his keys. "It's been a while since I beat that smug face of yours."

I stood there knowing that he was going to hurt me, possibly rape me again, but it was going to be worth it. When my door swung open, I started to tear up. Not because he had that murderous rage in his eyes that normally scared me, but because I could see Emma right behind him. She looked scared, tired, and had tears streaming down her face when she met my eyes.

I gave her a small nod, hoping she remembered to keep quiet no matter what. Emma was too gentle and soft for this shit. She'd never be able to handle what I was about to go through.

Right before he slammed the door, I saw Emma mouth *I love you*, and that alone let me know that I had done the right thing. I flew across the room, but was stopped by my chain as it caught my ankle. I fell to the ground, face first, and felt blood pool in my mouth. He took the chain and dragged me back to him, laughing.

"You just never learn when to shut up, do you?" He reached down, lifted me by my hair, and threw me against the wall. "I'm starting to think you love our time together."

I spat the blood out of my mouth and onto his face. "Oh yeah, it's not a fucking party without you." I sneered, taking advantage of his moment of shock as he wiped his face, and slammed my fist into his gut. He stumbled back and clutched his stomach, looking at me with pure rage.

"You have no sense of self-preservation, do you?" he asked, stalking toward me.

"Better to die on my feet than beg on my knees," I growled, right before he hit me again.

He lifted me by my throat and slammed me to the ground. "It's a great theory to test," he spat, lowering his head and licking the side of my face. Soft stars clouded my vision as I felt his hand lower down my body and between my legs.

"I know what you want, and it's not going to happen," I said, pushing through my fogged mind.

"Oh, really?" he chuckled, pulling the zipper down on my tattered jeans, forcing them down along with my underwear. "And what is that?"

I looked at him square in the eyes, and grinned. "You can't fucking break me. No matter how hard you beat me, or how many times you rape me, you fail to realize one thing—I don't *have* a breaking point."

He stopped gripping my throat and just glared at me, his chest rising and falling in anger. I decided to push my luck and kept going, looking down at his semihard member, and laughed.

"You can't even get it up, can you? You can't even fuck a woman unless she's crying or—"

"You shut the fuck up!"

"—damn near unconscious," I continued, ignoring his outburst. "That's why you were able to have me that one time, but you can't now, huh?"

"I said shut the fuck up, you fucking whore," he screamed, taking me by the throat again and shaking me.

I couldn't help but laugh. I did it. I found his weakness and cut it open for everyone to hear.

"Stop it! Stop fucking laughing," he yelled, but his pathetic tantrum just caused me to laugh even harder.

He got off me and pulled up his pants, turning his back to me. He walked over to the door and rested his hands against it, his breathing labored. I allowed the feeling to wash over me; I was beating him at his own game. The fact that I knew I was hitting a major nerve caused me to laugh so hard that I had tears running down my face. I stood and braced myself against the wall. I didn't know why I was acting this way, but I didn't have it in me to stop.

Without saying a word, he swung open the door and left my room, slamming the door behind him and locking it. Not even thinking, I started to walk forward.

"What, can't handle the truth?" I bellowed, and then grimaced as the chain pulled against my sore ankle. I grew annoyed and kicked my chained leg out, wishing I could go bang against the door as I heard his footsteps move up the stairs, but then I felt my chain go slack and I stopped. I turned to see that the plaque had pulled away from the wall. I walked over to it, and with a little effort, pulled it the rest of the way out.

"Well, I'll be goddamned," I whispered to myself in disbelief.

Emma waited until he was back upstairs and the music turned back on before speaking out.

"Lee, oh my God, are you okay?"

Still looking at the plaque in my hands, I smiled, nodding to myself. "Ladies, it's time to get the fuck out of here."

Twenty-Six Days Missing
—Richard

"Don't fucking give me that shit, Noah, I know you know something," I yelled, feeling my whole body shake.

Adam, Sadie, Luke, and I were all staying at the hotel where my parents had set up temporary residence. One of the hardest things I had ever done was to call my parents and tell them Emma was gone. The news had crushed them. My dad had to sedate my mom just so she would stop screaming. With the girls' apartment now a crime scene, and my apartment too small for all of us, my parents asked us to stay with them. I think they felt better having us around. We were gathered in the living area, getting our daily briefing from Noah.

"They are doing the best they can," Noah said with a steady voice to all of us in the room.

"That's horse shit," Luke said.

"Watch your tone," Noah said. "There are people everywhere looking for them."

"Well, they're just wasting their time because you know as well as I do that this Thomas kid has something to do with it." I crossed my arms and gave Noah a look, daring him to deny it.

"No, we don't know. Just because you have convinced yourself of something, because of your gut feeling, it's going to get you in trouble if you go out there snooping around. Maybe even killed."

"But Thomas does have something to do with this. You wouldn't be worried about us being around him if he wasn't," Adam said quietly.

Six pairs of eyes looked at him in shock. Adam hadn't spoken a word since he found out Emma was missing. Everyone had reacted with some form of distress, but not Adam. He just sat in silence, deep in thought. It was as if he had retreated into himself.

"I'm not sure, but I recently overheard some information that doesn't mesh with the story Thomas gave Chase," Noah replied. "But until they have more on the guy, there is nothing they can do."

"Fine, then who's David?" I asked, clenching my fists.

Noah sighed and shook his head. "I can't say."

Before I had a chance to call *bullshit,* Adam was out of his chair, across the room, and had Noah pinned against the wall by the neck.

"Answer the question," Adam shouted. Luke and I rushed forward and tried to pull him off, but his hand was locked around Noah's neck. "Answer us or I swear to God . . ."

"Adam, he can't breathe," I said, watching Noah's face turning bright red. Luke pulled on Adam's arm. "Come on, let him go."

He let go and stood back, watching Noah slide down the wall and onto the floor. Noah rubbed at his neck and coughed as Adam stood before him, his breathing erratic. He knelt down and pushed his index finger into Noah's chest.

"If she dies, it's on your hands, and I will spend the rest of my life reminding you of that," he growled. He got up quickly, grabbed his jacket, and walked out the door.

"Have you all forgotten that Lee is my sister, too? That I am just as destroyed as the rest of you?" Noah yelled. He looked at me and let out a deep sigh. "Richard, it's not that I don't want to . . ."

"You want us to stay out of it, but I can't. It's my sister and the love of my life out there," I said, grabbing my jacket and following Adam. I ran out to the parking lot just in time to see him getting into his car. "Adam!"

He turned and looked at me. "If you're coming with me, then we're doing this my way."

I nodded and got in the car. My phone buzzed in my pocket, but I ignored it. "What are we doing?"

Without saying a word, Adam put the car in gear and sped off. I waited until we were outside the city before I spoke. "We're going to Noah's?"

"Yeah, well . . . didn't you say his house was a shrine of information?"

I nodded. "I thought you'd just want to go straight to Nederland."

He tightened his hand around the steering wheel and growled. "That depends on what we find at Noah's house."

—⁓—

"You know the best thing about Noah living in a small town? He never locks his windows." I laughed as I popped open Noah's back window and crawled in. Adam laughed and hopped in after me.

We were quick to start going through all the folders, scattered papers, and pictures that lined the kitchen and living room. Adam was in the living room while I stayed in the kitchen. I almost lost it when I found the crime scene photos of the two girls they'd found. It looked like something out of a horror movie. They were naked, bloody, and disfigured. I had to close my eyes and take a few deep breaths to compose myself. I couldn't allow myself to think that Lee or Emma could end up this way.

"Richard," Adam said from the other room, pulling me out of my small panic attack.

"Yeah?"

"Do you remember Tom's brother's name?"

And then it clicked. *Son of a bitch.*

Adam was waving a folder and smirking. "Got 'em."

Chapter 13

Day Twenty-Nine
—Lillian

His hands moved gently up my body, not allowing one inch of skin to escape his fingertips. I writhed against his touch as he shifted my legs higher, letting his body sink deeper inside me. I bit my bottom lip to hold back my cries, which were quickly approaching.

"No," Richard said, panting and thrusting into me with haste. "I want to hear you. I need to hear you."

I threw my head back and moaned when I felt his hot mouth attack my neck. Richard had always been so attentive when it came to sex. I shouldn't even call it sex. Richard had never called it sex. We never said we loved each other, but that was what we made—love.

"Oh God, Richard, please." I felt as if my release was right at the cusp of breaking through.

He didn't say anything, but continued to thrust into me harder. One hand tightened around my breast and squeezed. I felt his teeth against my neck, and I yelped when he bit my skin.

I chuckled lightly. "Richard, slow down."

"Wrong name, whore."

I opened my eyes to see not my Richard, but *him* and his dark, demon eyes glaring down at me. I went to reach out and hit him, but my hands were tied over my head.

"That's right, bitch, you're all mine," he said, laughing.

I opened my eyes and screamed, thrashing my arms all around me.

"Lee . . . Lee . . ." Emma said. "It's just a dream, honey. He's not here."

Of course he's not here, the chicken shit.

I guess my little outburst had scared him off. When I told the girls that the plaque fell off the wall, everyone seemed to have relaxed, except for Emma. She was still receiving daily visits from Number Two, who we had now learned was named Thomas.

After *he* left that day, Emma told us everything she knew about Thomas, confirming our suspicions that he worked for the athletic department at the university. I could tell that Emma's forced visits were becoming more and more stressful on her. She would cry for hours afterward, feeling as if she were cheating on Adam. She swore Thomas never hurt her, or even tried to force her to do anything against her will, but it was the fact that she had to sit in that room and pretend to care for him that caused her so much pain. It made me sick.

During Thomas' visits he would still check on all of us, making sure that we had food and water, but he seemed to always do it when we were asleep. Normally the sound of the music turning off would rouse me from my sleep, but he kept it on so we wouldn't hear him moving around. At least, that's what I thought. The guy seemed like an all right kid, and I believed Emma when she said he wasn't hurting her, but if he ever opened my door he was going to get a mouthful of steel plaque in his face. I wouldn't kill him, but I'd make sure he wouldn't be getting up anytime soon.

I used my newfound freedom to try figuring out how to break down the door. It was locked, of course, but it was loose. I tried kicking it down, throwing myself against it, even swinging the heavy plaque against the hinges to break it down, but it wouldn't budge. This motherfucker was becoming more annoying than the plaque.

"Lee, please, just give it a rest for a while," Anna asked. "My ears are killing me."

"At least it's drowning out the noise of Patsy," Kandace said.

The last few days had been filled with nothing but tension and questions. When was *he* coming back? What else did Emma know about Thomas? Was she sure she hadn't seen the other guy before? I could tell she was becoming annoyed, and I couldn't blame her.

I didn't have any questions for Emma. Unlike the other girls, I didn't have a need to know more about these men. Kandace had become obsessed.

She asked Emma every possible question you could think of about Thomas. What they talked about, how he dressed, if he shaved, things that didn't mean shit when it came to getting out of here.

Sara had become quieter than usual. She only spoke to Anna in whispers, and that was only to prove she was still alive. Anna felt that Sara was starting to fade away, and in time would stop answering her calls altogether. Anna was starting to feel that maybe *he* wasn't going to come back, and that my plan to get out would fail, but I wasn't worried. I could feel it in my bones that he would be coming back soon. He was never able to stay away from us for long. He needed this—like the air he breathed. And I would be ready.

My body was slowly healing itself, and I pushed myself to start exercising again. I did push-ups, sit-ups, squats, and even set the mattress against the wall to use as a makeshift punching bag. I had to be ready.

With every punch I landed on the mattress I would see his face. His dark eyes. *Punch*. His short brown hair. *Punch*. That grin he would have every time he hit me. *Punch*.

"You're dead," I yelled, punching the mattress as hard as I could. "I'm going to fucking rip your heart out." I lifted my chain and started swinging my plaque against the mattress. I ignored the onslaught of feathers that flew around me as I continued to slash away at my now-tattered mattress. "I hate you, I hate you, I hate you!"

I screamed and fell to my knees and clutched my chest. My heart felt like it was about to rip itself out of my chest.

"Lee, are you okay?" Emma asked.

I got up and let the plaque fall from my hands. "Ask me that after we get out of here."

I lifted my hands and closed them into tight fists.

I'm ready.

Twenty-Nine Days Missing
—Richard

Adam and I had been camped out on the edge of the Reed property for three days now. The Reeds owned a double wide at the bottom of a steep hill, which sat on a pretty open field. The two of us set ourselves up at the top of the hill where we could hide behind an array of thick trees and bushes. We had a tent set up a few yards back, hidden within the trees, and enough water and canned beans to last us a week. I wasn't worried, though. We weren't going to be here that long.

We decided it was for the best not to let my parents or Luke know where we were or what we were doing. We only turned our phones on to call Luke and see if he had heard anything.

"When are you two coming back?" he asked.

I had him on speakerphone so Adam could hear the updates on Noah.

"When we find the girls," Adam answered.

"Luke, I'll call you tomorrow unless something happens. Tell Mom and Dad I'm fine and not to worry." Every time I called Luke, the only thing he could talk about was how frantic Mom had been about Adam and I being gone.

"Yeah, as if anything I have to say at the moment means shit," he grumbled, hanging up the phone. I pulled my thick jacket tighter around me, shivering at the feeling of the soft snow that had started to fall. It was almost pitch black outside. The only light that we had was the bright moon that glowed overhead.

I knew Luke was having a hard time keeping our parents calm, but how could any parent stay calm in this situation? He'd left a voice mail yesterday letting us know that Noah had called to say a hiker had found the body of Linda Baker lying on the side of the road. Just like the others, her body had been beaten beyond recognition and she had been brutalized. Luke told us that Dad had to sedate Mom again when she heard the news on television.

I knew what I was doing was wrong. I should have at least called my dad to let him know I was okay, but we weren't playing by the normal rules anymore. This was about finding Lee and Emma; we wanted all of them, and we wanted the ones who took them.

I rolled my eyes when my phone went off again, turning it toward Adam and showing him it was Noah again. Noah was leaving a countless number of voice mails on my phone, yelling at Adam and me to turn up, or else. As always, I hit the ignore button on my phone and turned the thing off to conserve the battery. Noah wasn't stupid; he knew where he could find us. He knew we had broken into his house and taken his file on David Reed. If he wanted the two of us to come forward, then all he had to do was come to the Reed property and arrest David and Thomas . . . or send the Boulder

County Sheriff to come pick us up. We knew we were doing the right thing. The police were moving too slow, acting like they had all the time in the world. Adam and I knew better, and the body of Linda Baker proved that.

"Richard," Adam whispered, motioning toward the trailer house. I took out my binoculars and saw a dark Jeep pull up beside the small home. Thomas, and a tall man we didn't recognize, exited the Jeep and went straight into the house.

"You think that's David?"

"I have no doubt in my mind," Adam replied.

"So what do we do? Call Noah?" I asked, handing my binoculars to Adam so he could get a better look.

"Fuck Noah," he said on a growl. "Like I told you, Richard, we're doing this my way."

As Adam kept his eyes glued to the brothers below, I decided to pull out the folder we'd found at Noah's and look through it again. I had the damn thing memorized by now—both of us did—but for some reason I kept finding myself reading it like it was a best-selling novel.

Finding the folder on David Reed had been a blessing and a curse at the same time. David Reed was the older brother of Thomas. There was no record of a father, but they had a mother named Wendi who lived out of state. Noah had somehow recovered police reports accusing her of child neglect as far back as when David and Thomas were toddlers. One report stated that when the boys were examined, they showed signs of having been abused for years, and David seemed to have gotten the worst of it. The state had taken them from their mother and placed them with some out-of-state relatives for a year. During that time, Wendi Reed left her abusive ex-husband for a new one, but not before she proved she was stable enough to have the children back.

This routine had gone on for years until David and Thomas became legal adults. After that, David disappeared for a short time—it looked like Noah couldn't seem to find anything on him between the ages of eighteen and twenty-five—but Thomas lived his life pretty openly. He had worked odd jobs all over Colorado until he settled in Boulder, landing a full-time job at CU.

The mistake Thomas made was telling Noah that David was "down south" working security at a mine, because Noah checked. David was hired down in Canon City, an hour south of Colorado Springs, but relocated after having too many incidents between him and some of the women on the site. He had been moved to an abandoned mine called Black Rose, to stand security until further notice.

"Down south, my ass," Adam said.

We sat there, staring at the small house, waiting for something—anything —to happen. My watch let out a quiet beep, and I looked down to see that it was midnight. *Day thirty.* It had been thirty days.

I huffed. "What the hell are they doing in there?"

"Look, there's movement," Adam whispered.

I ducked down and, sure enough, Thomas and David were getting back into their Jeep.

"We need to get back to the car," I said, gathering our stuff.

"You don't think the girls are here somewhere?"

"In that tiny shit hole?" I asked, nodding toward the double wide. "No, but they might be driving to where they are. Come on."

—⁓—

We followed the Jeep at a good distance as there weren't many other cars around. After a while, Adam turned off his lights and relied on the moon and the distant taillights to light our way. He slowed down when the Jeep turned right and disappeared into the trees before us.

"I know where they're going," I said, reaching down between my feet and pulling David's folder out of my backpack. I flipped it open and pointed to Noah's notes. "The abandoned mine. We're at Black Rose."

Adam didn't respond, he just continued following David's Jeep until we could go no farther. "My car can't handle this type of road. We're going to have to walk from here."

"Wrong," I said, watching the taillights disappear in the distance. "We're going to have to run."

—⁓—

Day Thirty
—Lillian

There was a collective gasp when a soft rumbling vibrated overhead. I looked up and took a deep breath. I wrapped the chain around my fist, letting the plaque swing back and forth.

"I just want you all to know that I love you. All of you."

"Lee, please don't do this," Emma said, weeping. "They'll find us. Please, I beg you. Don't risk your life."

I tried to control my breathing as I heard the sound of footsteps coming down the stairs. *Better to die on my feet than beg on my knees.*

The main door opened, and I bit down on my bottom lip to stop my teeth from chattering. To say I was anything less than petrified would be a lie. This was going to go down in one of two ways: I was going to die, or he was. It was just about who wanted it more.

I walked silently toward the door when I heard the two of them walk in. I peeked through the bottom of the door and watched their feet move around.

"You have fifteen minutes with her," *he* whispered, his voice laced with venom. "Make it count." He sounded pissed, which meant he was either going to come in my room or go after Sara.

Emma's door opened and then closed after Thomas. I lay there against the ground, waiting on his decision. I heard him groan, and then he started to walk down the hall. *Shit, he's going after Sara.*

I stood up quickly at the sound of her door being unlocked, tightening my grip around the chain when her whimper echoed through the hall.

Taking a deep breath, I started the battle. "Come on, asshole, you know you want me first."

"Shut up," he said.

"Come on, dick, let's see if you can get it up this time," I said in an almost lustful tone.

Emma's sobs grew louder as he relocked Sara's door and started walking toward mine. He laughed. "You ever think maybe my dick just doesn't like being stuck inside something that feels like a piece of plywood?"

I wrapped another link of the chain around my hand and smiled. "Maybe third time's a charm, douchebag. I'll even fight back, just like you like it."

I walked to the wall next to the door, and pressed my back to it. *You can do this, Lee, you can do this.*

"I knew I'd get you to beg for me," he said, unlocking my door.

Chapter 14

Day Thirty

The whooshing sound the chain made as it sliced through the air let off a scream in my dark cell. The adrenaline that pumped through me was intoxicating as the plaque connected with his chest. The air escaped from his lungs in an explosive rush and he toppled over in pain. Taking a step forward, I swung the plaque again, this time hitting him across the face. His head snapped back as he flew backward into the hallway, falling against Emma's door, causing it to burst open. I was hesitant to walk out into the hallway, feeling like I was going to be punished for leaving my room. My heart pounded and my skin prickled with fear. This fueled my anger even more. He had damaged me, and I was going to return the favor. I pushed down the rising bile in my throat as I crossed the threshold into the hallway.

I gasped when a body rushed forward and crouched over *his* unconscious form. He looked up at me and I froze, my breath going still in my chest as my instincts tried to decide if it wanted to fight or take flight.

Thomas looked down at my chain, then over at Emma's cowering body in the corner, and then back at me. He reached into his pocket, pulled out a set of keys, and threw them at me.

"Here," he said. I caught the keys in my free hand and held them tight to my chest. "Take the others and go." I started for Emma first, but Thomas stood up and blocked me. "No, she is mine."

I shook my head and took another step toward Emma. "I'm not leaving without her."

Thomas scowled and placed his hands on either side of Emma's doorframe, blocking my view of her behind him. "Then you're not leaving," he said in a matter-of-fact way.

I took a few steps back into the hallway as Thomas came toward me. He had the same look in his eyes that *he* did. The look of malice and utter hatred. I shoved the keys into my pants pocket and lifted the plaque into my hand.

"Listen to me, Thomas, you don't need to do this," I said, still backing away from his pursuit.

He smiled. "We love each other, Lee. You could be a part of that. You could be her maid of honor or something."

"You're crazy. Emma would never want any of that with you."

His body grew still, and his eyes . . . I had never seen such blackness. Not even in *him*.

"Tom, please, don't hurt her," Emma yelled from her cell.

He closed his eyes and took a deep breath. "I'm sorry, Emma," he whispered, and then lunged at me.

I swung the plaque at him, hitting his arm, but it was like it didn't even faze him. He flew on top of me, knocking me to the floor and pinning me down. I struggled against him as he wrapped his hands around my neck, squeezing hard.

"I'm sorry, I'm sorry, I'm sorry," he said over and over, while all my blood rushed to my face. I scratched and clawed at him, kicking my feet everywhere and trying to get loose. Small white spots glazed over my vision, and at the same time, my brother came to mind.

"Noah, I don't need to learn this. There's plenty of security on campus and I'm not going to sign up for night classes. Freshmen orientation isn't for three weeks! Can we postpone this little lesson of your paranoia for another night?"

"Just give your brother some peace of mind, and follow my lead."

I laughed as I watched Noah take his jacket off and fling it on his couch. "Noah, I'm not going to pretend to fight you. I'll sign up for a kickboxing class or something if it would make you—" My brother flew at me and pinned me against the wall, cutting me off. He wasn't hurting me, but he was making it known that he was stronger by tightening his grip on my arms when I tried to pull away.

I had never once been afraid of my brother, but looking into his eyes at that moment and seeing the seriousness of the situation, well, I decided to stop joking and pay attention.

"*He's got you against a wall,*" Noah said, his voice calm. "*It's late and you two are all alone. What do you do?*"

"*I . . . um . . . kick him in the nuts?*"

Noah murmured something like 'God help me', and pushed himself flush against my body. "You can't because he's right on you, Lilly. What do you do?"

I tried to remember everything my brother had ever told me. Every conversation we would have after reading about a woman being attacked or mugged. What do I do? What do I do, what do I . . . slack!

I let my body go slack, which caused Noah to step back and bend his knees to keep me up. With this new space for my legs, it allowed me to kick at his right knee, and he fell onto his back.

He lay there for a second and then started laughing. "That's my girl."

I was shocked that I felt out of breath. I had been running track for years, but in those last few minutes with my brother, it felt like I had run ten miles. "I can't . . . believe . . . you just . . . did that . . . to me."

He stood up and shook his head. "You know why you're out of breath?" he asked, and I shook my head. "Because you always stop breathing when you're scared, Lee. You have to learn to control that. What if this happens?" he said, and before I knew it he had me on the ground with his hands around my neck.

"*He has you on the ground, all his weight is in his hands, and, Lee . . . he is going to kill you. What do you do?*"

My brother's words echoed through my mind as I looked into Thomas' eyes. And then I remembered.

"*Take away his sight first,*" I heard Noah's voice whisper to me.

Feeling the thick ring of keys digging into my side, I reached down and pulled them out of my pocket. I clutched a key between my first and second finger and jammed it as hard as I could into his right eye. He let go of me instantly, clutching his face in pain.

"*Take his breath,*" I heard Noah say, as if he were right there next to me.

With everything I had in me, I flung out my fist and punched his exposed throat. Thomas sank off to the side, still holding his face, his blood seeping through his fingers. Pulling myself up, I steadied myself on shaky legs and lifted the plaque in my hands over my head.

"*And if you can't get away, you make it so he can't come after you again,*" my brother's voice said, fading away.

I looked down at Thomas and gritted my teeth. "Burn in hell, you sick fuck."

I slammed the plaque down as hard as I could against his head. He instantly fell limp, and then everything was silent. I remained standing there, glaring at him, not quite knowing how to register what had happened. I had just taken a man's life.

Kneeling down, I slowly picked up the keys that were now covered in blood. I closed my eyes tight and shoved them back into my pocket.

"Lee?" Emma called out.

"I'm fine, but I think I just killed Thomas."

"Where's the other one?" Anna asked.

"Who gives a shit?" Kandace said. "Just get us the fuck out of here."

I went back into Emma's cell and stopped in the doorway. *He* was still knocked out, or dead, I wasn't sure. He had a massive slash across the left side of his face and chest, and I smiled down at him when I maneuvered around his body. "Loser."

Emma stood up and opened her arms to me. I fell into them with relief, willing away my tears even though I knew they'd come. We were holding each other so tight that it was becoming hard to breathe, but I didn't care. When I finally pulled away, I took her face in my hands.

"Did they hurt you? Tell me the truth," I asked, not even realizing until then that I was crying. Her head shook as I continued to question her. "Did he touch you, or make you touch him?"

"No, Lee, I'm fine," she said, pulling me back into her arms. "I'm just so happy you are alive. I thought he was going to kill you."

I don't know how long we stood there, just crying and holding each other, before Kandace called out again. "This is all very Lifetime-Channel worthy, but what part of 'Get me the fuck out of here' do you not understand?"

I pulled away from Emma and looked down at her chain. "I don't know how to get them off," I whispered. "There's no lock for a key."

"Why don't you at least unlock their doors," she said with a tearful smile.

I nodded and kissed her cheek. "Will you be okay alone?"

"I'll be fine, just"—she looked at *him* on the floor—"could you move that?"

I turned and looked over at the still unconscious body of our abductor. "I'll drag him into the room I was in." I shoved the keys back into my pocket and slowly walked toward him. Closing my eyes again, I bent down and took him by the ankles before dragging him across the hall into my room.

"What are you doing?" Sara called out.

"Securing the prisoner," I said, dropping his feet on the floor.

Anna spoke for the first time since everything had begun. "Lee, see if he has a cell phone on him."

I laughed for not thinking of that myself, then patted down the front pockets of his jeans with shaky hands. I did feel something, but it wasn't a phone. I reached in and pulled out another set of keys.

"No cell, just keys," I told the girls, standing up and walking out of the room. The keys were almost identical to the ones Thomas had. The only difference between the two was that *his* had a set of car keys on them.

The first door I unlocked was Anna's. I opened the door slowly and gasped at the tiny little woman sitting cross-legged on the mattress. She had short dark hair, wide dark eyes, and bruises all over her body. In the faint light from the hallway, I could just make out some burn marks. They slashed across her skin like zebra stripes. But what stood out more than anything was the round belly that protruded from her slim form.

She stood up and started walking toward me, smiling. "Lee," she said with a slight sob.

I flung open the door and walked toward her, crying. "Anna," I whispered, trying and failing at keeping the tears at bay.

We stood there crying for a short time before I pulled away, wiping my nose with my sleeve. "I'm so happy to see you."

"Ditto," she said with a smile. "And you look like hell, Lee." She lifted her hand and caressed my face. I looked down at her round belly and laid a hesitant hand on top of it.

"Anna, I'm—"

"Shh," she whispered, shaking her head with tears trickling from her eyes. "Go help the others. Make sure they're okay, too."

I smiled and nodded. I took her hand in mine and gave it a soft squeeze before running to the next door.

I found Sara balled up in the corner, rocking herself, when I opened the door. Her long blond hair covered her face, but it couldn't hide the black and blue welts on her skin. I walked to her and sat down, engulfing her in my arms. She didn't even look at me, just wrapped her arms around my neck and started to cry. She felt so small and fragile against me, and yet so heavy with her pain. I wished I could have held her all night, if only to ease some of her pain, but I also had to see to Kandace. When I pulled away, Sara held me even tighter.

"I'll be back," I promised, smoothing my hand over her hair. "I'm going to check on Kandace, okay?" She nodded and released me with effort.

I stood up and crossed the hall to Kandace's room. I unlocked the door and smiled at the sight before me. She stood there, arms crossed, tapping her foot on the floor.

She smiled back at me. "Saved the best for last?"

"You know it, babe." We collided into each other's arms, laughing and crying at the same time.

"Sorry for being a bitch," she whispered.

"Sorry for taking so long to get to you."

Kandace chuckled against my shoulder and took a shaky breath. "Look at us, two tough bitches crying like a couple of babies."

"Your secret's safe with me."

Kandace pulled away, dried her eyes, and looked down at the chain still connected to my ankle. "Plan on taking a souvenir?"

I sighed and shook my head. "I don't know how to get it off."

"Bolt cutters?" Kandace shrugged.

"Yeah, let me run over to the store and get some," I said.

"Yeah, fuck you, too," she said. "Well, you're just going to have to go find some help. It's not like we're going anywhere."

I pulled her into my arms and squeezed her tight. "I'll be right back, I promise."

"I know," Kandace whispered.

I moved out into the hallway and walked past Thomas' body, making sure he was still dead. Then I went over to where *he* still lay, also to make sure he hadn't moved. I wanted to lock him in the room, but the doorknob must have broken sometime during my attack. I didn't want to leave the girls, but I knew I had to go get help.

"I'm going up to find some help," I said so they could all hear me. "I promise I won't be gone long."

I poked my head into Emma's room and met her eyes. "I love you."

"I love you, too," she said.

I went to the heavy metal door blocking the stairwell and fumbled with each key until I found the one that unlocked it. It took all my weight to pull the door open and, when I did, a gust of wind flew in. I could smell the forest and took a deep breath. Looking at the many metal stairs that rose in front of me, I didn't know what I'd find at the top of them, but I said a silent prayer and made my first step toward freedom.

Thirty Days Missing
—Richard

It took us almost an hour to hike the rough terrain heading toward Black Rose mine, with only the flashlight of our cell phones for light. I could feel it in my bones that we were where we needed to be. I wanted to just run up, find this asshole, and kill him with my own bare hands, but Adam was holding me back.

He sighed, shaking his head. "Look, Richard, I want nothing more than to go up there and beat the living shit out of them, too, but we've got to be smart. We don't know what we're walking into."

I looked at him and gritted my teeth. "Do you think I don't know that?" I quickened my pace and kept moving forward. "He has them, Adam. He has them up here, hungry, abused, and broken. I'm tired of waiting and I'm tired of being tired."

Adam sped up to catch me and grabbed my shoulder. "I understand you're scared and angry, and there is nothing wrong with that. I am, too, but we just have to be smart and careful. That's all I'm saying."

I knew Adam was right. We had to wait and see what happened, but it was killing me to know that these two assholes could have my sister and Lee stashed away somewhere in some abandoned mine. It was becoming almost unbearable.

We finally made it to David's Jeep and moved around the rocky area trying to find them, but they were nowhere to be seen. We even found the entrance to the mine, but it was caved in. I looked around and saw nothing but dark trees, rocks, and old wooden buildings that looked like if you sneezed on them they'd fall over. But there was nothing. We couldn't hear any voices, footsteps, or echoes. It was as if they got out of their car and disappeared.

"Do you see anything?" Adam whispered.

"No, it's too dark. All I can see is . . ." I stopped when I saw some movement near the entrance of one of the old worn-down buildings. The figure was small, a lot smaller than the two assholes we had seen earlier. *No, that can't be,* I thought to myself.

Without even giving Adam a second thought, I made my way down the road, through the scattered rocks, toward the figure. Still keeping out of sight, I watched the form hobble toward the Jeep parked by the side of the road. Her name escaped from my lips like a whisper, but it was as if she heard me because she turned in my direction.

"Who's there?" Lee said, her voice sounding tired and frail.

I dropped my backpack and started toward her. At that moment the dark clouds overhead seemed to have taken pity on us and moved away from the moon. I almost stopped in my tracks when the soft moonlight bounced off Lee's skin. She looked like she had been beaten within an inch of her life. The right side of her face was swollen, and her left eye almost looked black. She smiled at me and whispered my name. It was the most beautiful sound I had ever heard.

I raced toward her, seeing how hard it was for her to walk. Then I noticed the chain she was dragging behind her. She was just a few feet from me when, out of the corner of my eye, I saw a flash of movement in the shadows.

"No! Lee, get down," I said when I saw the gun rise up from David's hand and point toward her.

It was as if she didn't hear me. She just kept limping toward me with a smile on her face. I ran toward her as fast as I could, but when the sound of the gun rang through the air, I found myself on the ground with Lee lying limp in my arms.

He shot her. He fucking shot her.

"B-baby," I whispered, looking down at her frail body. "Baby, open your eyes."

I rocked her back and forth, waiting to see those beautiful blue eyes open up for me, but they didn't. I heard a hammer being cocked and I looked up to see the barrel of a gun pointed straight at me. I closed my eyes and pulled Lee's limp body closer to mine.

"I love you," I whispered as the sound of the gun went off.

Chapter 15

—Richard

I sat there with Lee in my arms, chanting in my head over and over again to God, thanking Him for letting me hold her in my arms one last time before I died. Every touch, every kiss, every soft word Lee had ever blessed me with, passed through my mind as the sound of the gunshot echoed through the trees.

"Richard?" I heard Lee whisper. I looked down to see her round blue eyes looking back at mine. She lifted her hand and touched my face. "It's really you."

Regretfully, I tore my eyes away from Lee to see Adam standing over David's twitching body. You could see the smoke seeping from Adam's gun, which was still clutched in his shaky hand.

"Adam," I said, trying to pull him out of his daze. He blinked at the two of us and then was at our side in an instant.

"Where did he shoot her?" he asked.

Lee gasped as I turned her body over, already knowing it was somewhere on her back.

"Shit," he whispered, standing up and pulling out his cell.

"Emma," Lee said, gasping in pain as I laid her flat on the ground.

"Where, Lee? Where is Emma?" I asked, taking off my jacket and laying it over her.

"In there," she whispered, pointing to the worn-down house. "Underground."

I glanced at Adam and he nodded, handing me the cell phone before running straight for the shack. Looking back down at the phone, I saw that he had dialed Noah's number. Noah answered on the first ring, his voice a growl.

"Where are you two?"

"Noah, it's Richard. We found them, all of them."

"Where are you?" he asked again.

"At an abandoned mine called Black Rose. Please hurry. Lee's been shot," I said, and then dropped the phone on the ground. I knew it was wrong to end a call that way, but Lee was starting to drift off again.

"Lee, baby, stay awake," I said, feeling tears escape my eyes. I tried as hard as I could to hold back my sobs when her eyes started to flutter.

"Richard," she said in such a hushed tone.

I held her hand in mine and stroked her bruised face. "I'm here, baby. I'm not letting you go. Not ever."

She lifted her bloodied hand and motioned for me to lean in. I moved in closer to hear what she needed to say.

"I love you," she whispered.

I gasped and leaned down, kissing her lips with my tear-soaked ones. "I love you, too, Lee," I said. "With everything that is in me, I love you. So much."

I leaned my forehead on hers and let my pain take over. I wanted to be strong for her, to look her in the eyes and tell her everything would be all right, but I couldn't. I was just thankful to have been able to tell her how much I loved her while I still had the chance. I lay down next to her and cried as I watched my heart slowly drift away.

After some time, I heard yelling in the distance, but I ignored it. It was as if everything had faded away. Lee was fading away, and all I could do was pray that God would show mercy on me, and take me, too.

I caressed the side of her face as she slept. We were facing each other, still sweaty from another mind-blowing lovemaking session. She fell asleep almost as soon as I eased out of her, a hushed moan of disappointment escaping both our mouths at the absence of the connection. Sometimes I would pull her against my chest, needing her body as close to mine as possible, but this night I wanted to see her face. I could have lain there for days, just looking at her angelic face. The only thing I needed was for her eyes to open. I knew that if they did, I wouldn't be able to hold myself back from ravaging her again, but she needed her rest, so I let her be.

"You are so beautiful," I whispered, trailing my finger from her rosy cheek to her full lips. She never stirred or pulled away, but like always, leaned toward my touch. Even in her sleep. "I wish I could tell you this when you're awake, but you know me—overthinking shit, as always." I let my finger move over to her hair and played with a strand that was curled in between us. "I wish I had the guts to tell you how much I love you. Not a day goes by when I don't think about you at least a hundred times. I dream of marrying you, making a family, and growing old with you.

"I hate myself for waiting so long to kiss you. The time I wasted, being afraid you'd say no and push me away." I stopped and took a deep breath. "I love you, Lillian Locke, and I want to spend the rest of my life making you happy."

I didn't mean to say it as loud as I did, so when she mumbled a little and scooted closer to me, I couldn't do anything but hold my breath and wait.

"Richard," she whispered, and then fell back to sleep.

I exhaled and pulled her to my chest. "Right here, baby," I whispered, letting my exhaustion take over.

A man's voice pulled me away from my memories. "I said move away from the girl."

I ignored his outburst. "I promise, baby. I'm not letting you go."

Hands reached under my arms and pulled me away from Lee's limp body.

"There's blood on him," said a woman.

I struggled against them, but everything felt like a blur until I heard one of them call out.

"Down here! They're all down here."

I went to sit up, but the woman looking me over pushed me back down to the ground.

"Where is he hurt?" the male voice asked.

"I can't find any wounds. I think he's just in shock."

I turned my head toward Lee and watched as two paramedics worked on her. She wasn't moving, she wasn't breathing, she was just—

"We got a pulse!" one of them yelled.

"Come on, Miss, hang in there," the other paramedic said as he placed a breathing tube down her throat.

She's alive.

Someone sat me up and shone a light in my right eye. "Sir, can you tell me your name?"

"Richard," I said, still not taking my gaze off Lee.

He nodded and moved the light to my left eye. "Can you tell us if you have been injured in any way?"

Injured? The love of my life has been shot, and is fighting for her life, hanging on by a thread. I'm not injured, I'm fucking destroyed.

"No," I replied.

"Well, Richard," the paramedic said. "We're going to have to take you to the hospital anyway. The police will meet you there to ask you some questions."

I didn't respond. My only thoughts were of Lee. I watched as they lifted her onto the gurney, moved her to the ambulance, and drove away. This was not how it was supposed to happen. It wasn't supposed to be her in there. It was supposed to be me. Hadn't she gone through enough?

"He's stabilized; let's get a gurney."

For a second I thought he was talking about me, but I realized he wasn't when they rolled the bed over to David. *That fucker is alive?* I didn't even know I was running toward him until three police officers pulled me back and held me down.

"He fucking shot her! He doesn't deserve to live. He's a murderer, and you're just going to save him?"

Cold steel wrapped around my wrists as I continued to scream.

—///—

Ambulance after ambulance arrived and parked outside the abandoned cabin after I was thrown in the back of a police car. Lee and David Reed's ambulances were long gone, and I was pissed. Pissed that they were trying to keep David alive, and pissed that I wasn't with Lee where I belonged.

The third ambulance to leave was Emma's. I watched as they carried her out of the building with Adam at her side, and took off before I could even get their attention. The officer who cuffed me then made his way toward the car when another man waved him over. It was Chase. They exchanged words before Chase came over and opened my door.

"Are you injured?"

"No."

He looked up at the officer and slammed the door.

"Take him to the precinct. He's not injured and I need answers."

Hours later, Adam joined me in the interrogation room where I'd been dumped. I walked right up to him and wrapped my arms around him for a tight hug. I didn't care how weird we might have looked at that moment, I was just happy to see that he was okay. He told me that Emma was fine and at the hospital with the others. When I asked how Lee was doing, he just shook his head and shrugged. Chase came in soon after and was quick to start drilling us with questions.

"So let me get this straight, you two broke into Officer Locke's house, stole confidential files, and decided to camp out on the suspect's property?"

"If you're looking for an apology, then you're wasting your breath," Adam said. "If it wasn't for us, those girls would either still be down there, or dead." He sat back in his chair and crossed his arms, closing himself off like he normally did when he was pissed.

"You're probably right, but that doesn't mean you guys can just do whatever you want," Chase said. "You should have called us the second you saw David Reed pull up, but instead you shot him in the back! It's hard to arrest someone when they're stuck in surgery fighting for their life."

"Can you honestly tell me that you care if this prick lives or dies?" I asked, gritting my teeth. "You had his brother, and you let him go. Excuse me if I don't give a rat's ass if we stepped on your toes."

"It's called obstruction of justice, boys, and where did it get you? A man is dead, and two more people are fighting for their lives from gunshot wounds."

"We had nothing to do with Thomas' death," Adam said. "He was already dead when I went down there."

"And like I told the officer who brought me in, Lee was already above ground when Adam and I saw her, and David was pointing a gun at her. If Adam hadn't shot him, then she'd be dead right now. We all would be."

"You two still have a lot to answer for," Chase said.

I slammed my elbows on the desk and rested my head in my hands. I was beyond annoyed with all of this. Lee and my sister were in the hospital, and I was here. *To hell with this.*

"Look," I said, glaring at the man who was fast becoming my least favorite person in this world—second only to the fucking asshole who should have died at that mine. "Unless you or Officer Locke plan on pressing charges for us breaking into his house, I'm not answering any more fucking questions."

"I agree," Adam said. "Anything more will require an attorney present." He then looked over at the mirror and flipped it off. "And that goes for all of you watching back there, too."

Agent Chase stood up fast, causing his chair to fall back onto the floor. I looked up and rolled my eyes as he bent over the desk and glared at us.

"They could have all died because you two wanted to play cowboy for a day. You could have died, too. I hope you both understand that because of you two, we'll probably never know the full story." He ran his hands over his face. "Go. Be with your girlfriends, but understand that this isn't over."

Adam and I didn't answer; as soon as we heard the word *go*, we were out of our chairs and out the door. Once we got our belongings back, I called Luke to pick us up.

———～～～———

Luke told us as soon as we got in the car that Lee was in surgery, and Emma was sedated, as were the other girls. They had all been placed in a quiet and very secluded area in the hospital, receiving much-needed medical attention and rest.

"Richard?" Luke said, moving his eyes from the road to look me over.

"Yeah?"

"You're covered in blood, little bro."

I looked down at myself. I hadn't paid attention to my appearance until he pointed it out. "It's . . . um . . . it's not mine," I said, running my hands through my hair.

"Is it his?" Luke asked next, tightening his grip on the steering wheel.

"No, there would be more," I replied. Which was true. If I had killed him, it would have looked like I had bathed in it.

"Then—"

"It's Lee's, Luke," Adam said. "Let's just get to the hospital."

When we finally crested the hill and the hospital came into view, there were nothing but flashing lights, news vans, and reporters everywhere.

"Oh yeah, the vultures showed up less than an hour after they all got here," Luke said, flipping them off as we drove by the crowd.

Lee and Emma didn't need this. None of them did.

Luke led the way through the parking garage and the endless halls until, finally, I saw my parents up ahead.

"Mom!"

She turned, and the look on her face almost made me want to turn around and walk in the opposite direction. "Shit."

"You have no idea," Luke whispered.

"Thanks for the warning, jerk."

I stopped walking when my mother started coming toward me. Her face was puffy and red, from crying most likely, and she looked like she hadn't slept in days. Adam and Luke stood back as my mom reached up and slapped me across the face.

"Don't you ever do that to me again," she said, and then pulled me into a tight embrace. She sobbed into my neck as I wrapped my arms around her and rocked her back and forth.

"I'm sorry, Mom. I promise," I whispered into her hair. I felt her nod against my neck, and I smiled in relief. I deserved way more than just a slap in the face for what I had put her through, but I would do it all again knowing I'd get my girls back. "It was all Adam's idea," I said, before burrowing my face in her hair.

"I heard that, you dick," Adam mumbled.

~✺~

It had been three days and Lee was still in a medically induced coma after her surgery. They had started taking her off the medication, and we were expecting her to wake up at any time. You would think from the amount of stuff in her room that Lee was on her deathbed. Flowers were stacked everywhere, cards were taped on the walls, and tons of gifts lined the small hospital room floor. Noah and I joked how Lee would hate all this attention.

She was never left alone. Sadie and Noah would switch every twelve hours so they could eat and sleep, but neither of them ever looked like they actually had. As for me, I had yet to leave. I showered, slept, and ate in the hospital. Everyone had begged me to get out and breathe some fresh air, but I couldn't. I'd promised Lee I would stay with her, and I planned on keeping that promise. Although I was itching for a cigarette.

A day ago, the FBI had held a press conference to confirm that the girls had been found and that the suspect was in custody. What they had failed to mention was that the asshole was upstairs, in a different area of the hospital, recovering from the bullet wound that should have ended his life.

"Richard?"

I turned to see a young nurse standing in Lee's doorway. "Yes?"

"There is someone who would like to meet you," she said.

I glanced over at Noah, who looked as tired as I felt. "I'm good," he said. "My mom will be here soon to switch with me."

I nodded and then followed the young nurse down the hall to where I knew the other girls were staying. She opened one of the doors, gave me a small smile, and stepped aside. I walked into the dimly lit room and recognized Anna. I had each of the girls' names and images ingrained into my memory. And Noah told me that when he had spoken to Anna, she'd told him that she and Lee had become close during their time together. I hadn't planned on meeting her or any of the girls until Lee was awake, but who was I to turn down her request?

"Wow, you are a cutie," she said, smiling. "Lee spoke about you all the time, but her words didn't do you any justice." She ran her hand over her large belly and sighed. "How is she?"

"Stable," I said, scratching the back of my neck, unsure of how to respond to her compliment. "She's supposed to wake up any moment." I motioned toward the chair next to her bed. She nodded and smiled. "So how are you holding up?"

She waited until I sat down before answering. "Better, I guess." She rubbed her belly again, and I could see her eyes gloss over a little. "It's a girl."

"I'm sorry," I whispered, unsure of what to say. "Have you decided if—"

"If I'm going to keep her?" she answered, wiping her eyes. "I don't know yet, but I already know what I'm going to name her if I do."

"Really?"

"I'm going to name her Lillian. It feels right. Without Lee, we wouldn't be here." She gave me a short glance, her eyes nervous with what I had to assume was a look for approval.

I nodded and smiled. "I think she would feel honored."

"No, she will be annoyed, but she'll get over it." Anna laughed, and I joined in.

Yep, she knew Lee all right.

There was a long pause, and I could tell by the look on her face that she wanted to say something. I cleared my throat and leaned forward in my chair. "Anna, I can't tell you how sorry I am for what happened to you, but I need to ask you something."

"Okay."

"I can't imagine what went on down there, but I need to know, is she going to be my Lee when she wakes up?" I felt like shit for asking this, but I had to know.

"Does it matter?"

"No, I will love her no matter what, but I want to be prepared, for a lack of a better word."

Anna nodded and took a deep breath. "Each of us were hurt in different ways." She wiped the tears that pooled at the corners of her eyes. "Lee . . . well, *he* punished her for giving us hope. She was always picking fights with him so he would hurt her and not one of us. She blames herself for Ruth's death."

I held my face in my hands, trying to hold back the sobs that threatened to take over. The pain she must have gone through, the suffering. I don't know why, but I had to know more. "Did he . . . did he rape her?"

"No one was spared," she whispered. "Except your sister."

I felt my body start to shake as my tears spilled over. Anna didn't say another word, and for that I was grateful. I didn't think I could handle hearing much more.

"*Doctor Kent to room 233, stat*," a voice blared in the hallway.

"That's Lee's room," I said, standing up and wiping my eyes.

"Go," Anna said.

When I turned the corner, I could hear Lee's screams echoing down the hallway. I ran into her room and was dumbfounded by the number of nurses and doctors that were trying to hold her down. She was thrashing around as they tried to tie her wrists and ankles to the bed.

"What are you doing?" I yelled.

I pushed one of the doctors away and held Lee's face in my hands. "Lee, look at me," I said. Her eyes were wide, wild with fear, and tears were streaming down her cheeks. She kept looking around everywhere except at me. "Lillian," I said a little louder. "Look at me." Her eyes moved to mine and she instantly stopped fighting.

"Richard?" she whispered, sounding stunned.

"Yes, baby," I said. "You're safe. You're in the hospital. You were shot."

Fresh tears started to trickle down her face as she raised her hand to cup my face. "You're here," she said, almost sounding surprised.

"Of course I'm here," I said, smiling. I leaned forward and rested my forehead against hers. "Nothing will ever keep me away from you again. I love you too much to be away from you."

"I love you, too," she said, sniffling and wrapping her arms around my neck.

I turned my head and saw Noah ushering the doctors and nurses out of the room. I nodded when he mouthed that he would be right outside.

I held Lee softly, so as not to hurt her, as she sobbed against my neck. "Shh, baby, it's all right. I've got you, and I'm never letting you go." I felt her nod and take a few deep breaths.

"Where's my mom and Noah?"

I pulled back and kissed her cheek. "Noah is right outside, and your mom is on her way. She went to get food for all of us. She'll be so upset that she wasn't here for you."

"And the girls?" she asked, looking very serious all of a sudden.

"They are all here, resting. Some of them are even being discharged soon," I said. "Emma is leaving today. She will be happy to know you are awake. She's been asking about you."

She didn't smile. She just nodded and bit at her lip. "And what about . . . him?"

I found myself hesitating, unsure of how to answer. "He's upstairs. Adam . . . uh . . . Adam shot him. He's recovering from surgery, and the police are guarding him around the clock."

Her eyes shot up at mine. "I want to see him."

"What? Why?" *Why would she want to ever see him again?*

"I just have to," she whispered, sitting back in her bed with a hiss.

"Are you okay? Are you in pain?" I panicked, searching for the nurses' button.

"I'm fine. I don't feel too much." She yawned.

I leaned forward and kissed her forehead. "Sleep, baby. I'll be here when you wake up."

She looked up at me with tears swimming in her eyes. "Richard, I'm afraid."

I took her hand in mine and kissed her fingers. "Of what, baby? What are you afraid of?"

"I'm afraid that I'm going to fall asleep and not wake up again. I'm afraid I'm going to wake up and I'm going to be in the dark. I'm afraid . . . I'm just afraid, and I hate it. I am just so tired of being afraid."

My chest hurt as I listened to her confession and wished I could take that fear and pain away from her.

"Sleep, baby," I said, kissing her hand again. "Sleep, and I promise I will make sure there will be a tomorrow."

I sat down in a chair next to her bed, giving her hand a soft squeeze, and kissing it one last time. She smiled and mumbled that she loved me. I told her I loved her, too, laid my head down next to her hand, and let sleep take over.

—

—Lillian

"The poor thing," a woman's voice whispered, rousing me from my dreamless sleep. "I can't imagine what they must be going through right now."

"I know," another woman's voice whispered back.

I kept my eyes closed, ignoring the soft pain in my back. I had developed a tolerance for pain by this point, and even though it was due to being chained up underground for weeks, I learned that tolerance can be an ally.

"If I had it my way, I would have let that psycho die on the operating table," one of them said.

"I just hope he gets put away for a long time so he can go away and never bother these poor girls again," the other one said.

There was some rustling around and then they started whispering again.

"Shouldn't we wake her? Doctor Kent wanted her to start moving around as soon as possible."

"In a minute. Let's add this to the computer and find her a good wheelchair."

I waited until they left the room before I opened my eyes. The room was dimly lit, the only sound coming from the steady beat of the machines around me. Richard was asleep in the chair next to me, his face buried in his arms as he rested against my bed. In the far corner, my mom was curled up like a cat on a small sofa bed. She seemed a lot more peaceful and relaxed than earlier when I woke up to her hysterical voice. Thank God Noah had been here to help calm her. I knew I looked bad, but getting *that* reaction from my mom made me realize I must have been worse off than I thought.

Slowly pulling myself upright, I swung my legs over the side of the bed and bit down on my lip to hold back the sting of pain that shot through my body. I looked down at my right arm and quietly removed the blood pressure cuff. Just as I was about to let my feet touch the ground, one of the nurses from before walked into the room.

"I know you ain't trying to walk on your own," she whispered, walking toward me. Her nametag said Tabby.

"Just seeing if I can do it," I said, producing the most sincere smile I could muster.

Tabby held on to my left arm to help steady me as I tried to make my way toward the bathroom. I hated having a damn needle in my arm. I'd have to drag the stupid IV stand everywhere.

"You seem to be doing pretty well, Miss Locke. Maybe I can get you a small walker to help you move around," she said.

I nodded and opened the bathroom door. "That would be great. The more mobile I am, the quicker I can heal."

When I walked in the bathroom, Tabby looked over her shoulder and then back at me. "I'll see if I can find one. Just don't forget to put the clip back on your finger when you go back to bed and I'll just hook up the rest when I get back."

I smiled. "I will. I promise."

Closing the door quickly behind me, and avoiding the mirror at all costs, I counted to twenty before peeking out into the room to see if Tabby had returned. She hadn't. Everyone was still where I left them. I walked to the other side of the bed where Richard was sleeping. As carefully as I could, I slipped the clip on his index finger, and then started to make my way out of the room with my IV bag in tow.

I opened the door quietly and peered out into the hallway. It was late, so I wasn't surprised to find the hallway empty. There was a thick wooden railing that lined the wall, and I used that to help me walk down the hall. When I reached the elevators, I was relieved to find an abandoned wheelchair sitting off to the side. Tossing my IV bag into the seat, I used it to help me into the elevator, and quickly pushed the up button, not wanting anyone to see me.

When I got to the third floor, I stuck my head out and made sure no one was around before making my way down the halls. After a few minutes, I almost gave up—until I saw a police officer sitting outside a room.

Found you.

How the hell was I going to get him away from that door? I looked around and contemplated pulling the fire alarm, but decided against it. It wasn't that I cared about getting caught; I just wanted to make sure I was done before I was caught. Looking around, I saw a small flower pot sitting on a table by some chairs. For a second I thought about hitting the cop on the head with it, but I threw it across the hall instead, cringing as the sound echoed everywhere. The pieces skidded to a stop and bounced off a few walls. I watched as the cop stood up from his chair and started heading toward the broken pot. As fast as I could, I rolled myself over to the door, opened it, rolled the wheelchair inside, and shut the door behind me.

Wow, Adam got you good.

He had wires, IVs, and tubes coming out of him from every direction. I smiled at the thought of him feeling some pain, but more than anything, knowing that he was going to be feeling a lot more real soon.

I wheeled over to the chart that lay on the small table by his bed. I picked it up and opened it.

"So your name is David," I said to myself. "You're a security guard for the mines." I looked over and spat on him. "Loser." I continued reading about him until I felt satisfied that I knew enough about who he was. I moved closer to him and noticed his wrists were handcuffed to the sides of the bed.

"Who's chained up now, bitch? Can you hear me, David?" I asked, giving him a light slap on the face. "Can you hear me in that fucked-up head of yours?" I slapped him again, hoping he could hear me. "I know what's going to happen once you get well. There's going to be a trial, and you're going to plead temporary insanity, and the girls and I will have to live in fear wondering if you'll ever get out and find us. Well, David, I'm here to tell you that isn't going to happen."

I reached up and tightened my hand around his breathing tube, cutting off his air supply. All I could see was Ruth's face as I watched the lines on the screen start to move erratically. I'm sure there had to have been beeping— maybe even alarms going off—but I didn't hear them. All I heard was the thumping of Linda's head as it was being dragged up the stairs. I could feel tears starting to sting my eyes, but I refused to let them fall. This was their peace. This was me fulfilling my promise to them.

"It's judgment day, asshole."

—◦—

Chapter16

—Lillian

They say time heals all wounds, but I didn't think I fell into that category anymore. I was once happy, safe, and carefree, but not anymore. Now I knew that every shadow, every sudden movement, every unfamiliar sound would be *him*, and his haunting memory. He had left his mark on me, on all of us, and no amount of time could remove that. We would all be that way. We would be sixty-year-old women, crying in our sleep, still afraid of the dark. His death wouldn't change that, but it would have been a start.

I didn't even hear the door burst open, or the yelling that filled the room, because of all of the scenes flashing through my mind.

Every cry of pain that echoed out when he hit one of the girls.

Hearing his lighter flip open.

Ruth's neck snapping.

Sara screaming for hours when he was done with her.

That fucking laugh he would bellow when he was raping us.

I could feel people around me, clawing at my hand as I squeezed tighter.

"Miss Locke, let go," a man yelled, but I wouldn't answer. If they wanted me to let go then they were going to have to saw my fucking arm off.

"Lee . . . Lee . . . let go," I heard my brother say.

Why is it when I hear my brother's voice in pain, the waterworks turn on like a damn flood?

I shook my head violently and maintained my grip. "He has to pay, Noah. He has to suffer," I cried, not taking my eyes off *him*.

"And he will, Lee. I swear to God he will," my brother whispered, moving closer to me.

"No, I'm not going to let some fucking lawyer get him off," I said. "He has to pay. It has to be me. I promised," I said a little more slowly, finding it hard to talk all of a sudden.

The room was becoming fuzzy and I was having a hard time holding on to the tube. I felt hands separating my fingers and pulling me away from *his* body.

"No," I slurred.

"It's okay, Lee, I got you," Noah whispered, kissing my forehead.

"I promised," I whispered, feeling the darkness take over.

—∿∿—

—Richard

Lee had to be sedated after what she did to David. The hospital wanted to strap her down to the bed, but Noah and I told them to go fuck themselves. She'd been chained to a fucking wall for thirty days, and the motherfuckers wanted to strap her down! *Idiots.* We settled instead for mild sedation so she would still be somewhat coherent but unable to move around without our help. She hadn't said a word since she had woken up from the first injection.

I woke up to the sound of alarms going off in the hallway, and I noticed Lee wasn't in her bed. I looked behind me and saw that Sadie was looking just as worried as I felt. I got up and ran to the bathroom, hoping that Lee was in there, but it was empty. When we walked out of the room, we saw a gurney being rolled down the hallway with an unconscious Lee on it.

"What the hell is going on?" Sadie said, spotting Noah talking to a doctor at the nurses' station.

"There was an incident," Noah said.

"Can you be a little more vague for me, Noah?" Sadie said. She turned to me and pointed toward the group of people that were pushing Lee down the hall. "Follow them and I'll catch up in a minute." She didn't have to tell me twice.

Lee was taken to a room at the end of the hall that was almost like her other room . . . almost. *The first thing that stood out was that the door was metal, and not wood. It also had a keypad on either side, which took me aback. 'Has David escaped? What's with the extra security?' I noticed Tabby, Lee's nurse, walking toward me, and I hoped she could give me some answers.*

"Tabby, what's going on?" I whispered.

She looked over her shoulder and leaned in to me. "Lee left her room, while you and her mom were sleeping, and went to his room."

"What?"

"She tried to kill him. Wrapped her hand around his respirator and cut off his air supply, but her brother distracted her long enough for a doctor to sedate her."

I looked into her room and saw the doctors starting to strap her down to the bed.

"Tabby, please, don't let them tie her down," I said. "She's been through so much already."

"I don't know, Richard. The hospital—"

"Tabby," I said, taking her hand in mine. "That monster chained my girl to a wall and raped her. She had to sit down there and listen to him do that to these other girls, too. She sat there, defenseless, as he killed her friends." I could feel the tears rolling down my cheeks. "Please, Tabby, I beg you, don't let her wake up tied down again."

Tabby was definitely going on the family Christmas card list from now on. Lee might not remember her, due to all the drugs they were pumping in her, but I'd never forget her. She had no idea what it meant to me to see her go in there and call those doctors stupid for tying Lee down. She pissed off a lot of doctors that day doing that, but as she put it, "They can kiss my fifty-year-old black ass." I developed a whole new level of respect for nurses that night.

I wasn't supposed to be staying overnight in Lee's new room, but Tabby took care of that for me, too. Lee would wake up every now and then, to eat and move around a little, but she never spoke. She wouldn't even acknowledge anyone, just nodding or shaking her head when asked a question. Sadie would leave the room to cry, and Noah would be gone for hours sometimes, always coming back smelling like smoke, but I couldn't find it in myself to leave her. She was my forever. When she was in pain, then I was in pain, too. Even though she wouldn't talk to me, or look at me, I knew she wanted me there. I held her hand and she squeezed back, and that was all the reassurance I needed.

The only time she seemed at peace was when she was asleep. I would stroke her hair and kiss her hand as she slept the night away. I caught myself singing to her all the time, never knowing why I started—it just felt right. I sat back in my chair and scooted as close to her bed as it would allow, still keeping a soft grip on her hand. I kept my voice low as I hummed a melody to her. I leaned forward, and left a soft kiss on top of her index finger, and rubbed the tip of my nose over it. I lifted my other hand and caressed the silky soft skin that was exposed around the tape that held her IV to her arm.

Lee stirred and shifted her body toward mine. I smiled a little, relieved that she still did that because, before all this happened, no matter how far away I rolled from her in bed, she always scooted toward me. I started humming again and I felt her hand tighten around mine. I leaned down and kissed it, resting my forehead against her hand.

"I love you, too, Richard," she whispered in her sleep.

A warm tear escaped my eye and landed on top of her cold hand.

"Forever, baby," I said, smiling as I let my eyes close so I could finally sleep.

—Lillian

I was released from the hospital earlier than expected so that I could go to Nina, Ruth, and Linda's memorial service. I didn't want to go, but I couldn't say that out loud. Everyone was making a very big deal about going and I didn't want to seem like a bitch for saying no. I had nothing against anyone who wanted to go—I loved these girls—but to me, a funeral was nothing but a depressing pot-luck. Sitting around and listening to everyone talk about how wonderful the deceased had been, then going somewhere to eat and cry. I didn't see the point. I already knew how wonderful and strong these women were. They were my sisters, and I loved them. I didn't need to stand around a bunch of strangers to prove that.

I hadn't spoken since my failed attempt at killing *him*. I couldn't even say his name. He had no name in my mind. He would always just be *him*. After they stabilized *him*, the detectives moved him to another hospital. I felt like such a failure. I was there. I held his worthless life in the palm of my hand. I wasn't going to choke this time, I wasn't going to make the same mistake twice, but I did.

No one spoke of it, and I appreciated that. I didn't need a reminder of my failure. Noah was the one to come into my room and explain to me that it never happened. The hospital staff and the authorities were turning a blind eye to the incident, and it would never be mentioned again. I guess I should've been grateful, but I wasn't. A part of me wanted him to know that when *he* was helpless, I had held his life in my hand. I should have just shoved a blunt object through his heartless fucking chest.

Emma and I hadn't been back to the apartment because the media had apparently set up shop on our street. Luke said the reporters had been interviewing everyone in the surrounding apartments for weeks now, and any time someone even went in the general direction of our door they were swarmed. A barricade had been put up, but the reporters didn't seem to care.

I was relieved when Richard's parents offered to get us rooms at the hotel where they were staying. Both my mom and brother insisted I could stay with them, but I wasn't ready yet. I knew they would just walk on eggshells around me, kind of like Richard, but worse. I wanted space, but at the same time, I didn't.

I didn't know how I felt.

The first night was the worst. After I got out of the shower and dressed, I stood there just looking at myself in the mirror for hours. It was the first time I had really looked at myself since . . . well, it had been a while. I didn't even recognize the woman looking back at me. Aside from the cuts, bruises, and fading black eye, I still couldn't see myself. It was as if I was looking at a stranger.

Richard had pulled me out of my thoughts with a soft tap on the door. His room was adjoining mine, so he was constantly checking up on me. I walked out to find the room softly lit and a picnic spread out on the carpet in front of the television. He was being supportive, thoughtful, and caring, and I felt like an utter bitch when I told him that all I wanted to do was sleep. The memorial was the next day and I knew I needed the rest. Being the wonderful man that he was, he smiled and nodded in agreement.

"It has been a long day, hasn't it?" he said. "Rain check?"

I smiled back and gave him a hug, thanking him for his thoughtfulness. I went to bed, leaving the lights and television on for obvious reasons, and drifted off to sleep.

Almost instantly, as if the moment I closed my eyes, I was back in that room and the sound of a steel guitar echoed around me.

No. NO! I got out!

I looked down at my ankle and saw the chain around it. "No, this isn't real. I'm going to count to ten and it's all going to go away."

The sound of footsteps coming down the stairs made me start to panic. "Anna! Kandace!" I shouted, but there was no response, no sound but the screech of the metal door and the haunting voice of Patsy Cline.

Keys jingled as the door closed, and the footsteps grew closer. I looked around for something, anything, I could use to defend myself from what was about to happen, but there was nothing.

"I fall to pieces, each time someone speaks your name. I fall to pieces. Time only adds to the flame."

I covered my ears to block out the heartbreaking lyrics as the footsteps stopped in front of my door, and I held my breath, and closed my eyes.

It's not real. It's not real. It's not real.

I heard the lock turn and the door being pushed open. I let out a shaky breath, opened my eyes, and cried out when I saw his silhouette in the doorframe. My body trembled when he reached behind his back.

"Nobody but you and me, whore." He pulled out a gun and aimed it at me. "I always save my favorites for last." He pulled the hammer back and sang along. "You walk by and I fall to pieces."

The echo of the gun ended with the song as the bullet whizzed toward me.

"Lee, Lillian! Wake up!"

I sat up in bed screaming and thrashing out at whoever was holding me. Even when I realized that it was Richard, I still pulled myself out of his grasp. I tumbled onto the floor, realizing that the room was dark.

"Why aren't the lights on?"

"I turned them off," he answered, his voice cautious.

"Why?" I yelled. "If I wanted them off I would have turned them off myself."

"I just thought—"

"No, if you had thought, you would have understood why I left them on," I said.

I went over to the wall and flipped the switch, causing the room to light up. I noticed Richard was still sitting on my bed in his pajamas, looking like I had just slapped him in the face. I turned away from him, not needing to feel guilty for lashing out at him. I covered my face with my hands and tried to force back the tears that were trying to escape.

"I just need the lights on, okay?" I whispered.

"Of course," he answered. I could hear him stand up and walk toward me. He didn't touch me, but I could feel him right behind me. It was as if his body was radiating some kind of calming influence on me. "I'm sorry," he whispered.

I turned and wrapped my arms around him, pressing my cheek against his strong chest and whimpering. "I'm sorry, too."

We stood there embracing and whispering how much we loved each other for what felt like hours, and for a small time, he helped me forget the pain.

I woke up in bed, still wrapped in Richard's arms, and it felt so nice. I didn't have the nightmare again, so I decided that if sleeping with Richard kept them away then he better get used to sleeping with the lights on.

Emma and the girls thought it would be nice if we all matched at the funeral, so Emma and her mom picked out black and white dresses for all of us. My mom did my hair, and Emma finished my makeup. Once we were all ready, we left by the back exit of the hotel. The media had been less than respectful toward us; it was almost as if they felt we owed them something. Luckily, we had a police escort for the forty-five-minute drive to Fairmount Cemetery.

We couldn't help but be grateful at how supportive they were being, but it all came with a price.

"Wow, Fairmount? That's pretty—"

Emma turned to Luke and gave him a dirty look. "Luke, don't even."

"What? I think it would be an honor to be put to rest next to so many historical figures."

Mrs. Haines huffed and crossed her arms. "Really, Luke? Keep it to yourself. This is neither the place nor the time."

"Sorry," he said, as the car pulled off to the side. I sat there for a minute, watching the flow of unknown faces pass by as they headed toward the three coffins at the top of the hill. I spotted the others right away, since we were the only mourners wearing identical dresses. They all smiled and hugged each stranger that approached; each unfamiliar face was probably a relative or close friend of one of our fallen sisters.

"Lee?"

I turned to see Richard extend his hand toward me. I took a deep breath and placed my hand in his.

"Just say the word and we'll go, okay?" he whispered, kissing the side of my head.

I slipped on my sunglasses and nodded, concentrating on putting one foot in front of the other as I followed my family to our seats.

It was eerie to look at the large blown-up pictures of Nina, Linda, and Ruth. The pictures made them seem so calm, so happy. A snapshot in the life of a girl that would never have existed again, even if they had survived. Emma, Anna, Kandace, Sara, and I all had white roses with us, and we walked by the caskets and dropped the flowers in the ground as they were lowered. I stood there watching my fallen sisters' caskets sink into the darkness and I found myself becoming annoyed at their families. These girls died in the darkness, and now they were being left there to rot. I felt a hand on my shoulder but I moved away, not wanting anyone to touch me.

"I'll just . . . give you a minute," I heard Richard say, and I turned around to see that I was the only one left standing there.

"Thank you," I whispered as he walked away.

I stood there and watched as the workers started shoveling the dirt over their caskets. I found it hard to breathe when I looked down and saw that I couldn't even see Ruth's casket anymore. I felt the tears start to roll down my cheeks as Linda's soon became consumed in dirt. I glanced at Nina's and nearly fell to my knees when I saw that her grave was almost full. I couldn't bear the thought of walking to the car yet, so I turned in the opposite direction and ran. I found a quiet spot and sat down, leaning against a tall tree. It seemed a good place to allow myself to have a much needed breakdown. I don't know how long I was there, but when I finally opened my eyes, the sky had already started to darken a little.

"Lee," a soft voice said. I looked over my shoulder and there stood my sisters. One by one, Emma, Anna, Kandace, and Sara came toward me, and sat down around me.

"We need to get drunk." Sara sniffled.

"Fuck that." Kandace laughed. "We need to get fucking wasted."

All the girls laughed.

"Well, I guess that makes me the designated driver." Anna sighed.

"Fuck yeah, Anna, that's the spirit." Kandace laughed.

Emma shrugged. "Why not? I think we've earned it. What about you, Lee?"

"Sure," I nodded. "We evaded death . . . I think we deserve it." Anything to help numb the constant feeling of failure that seemed to be wrapped around me.

While the girls went off with their families to get their things and let them know that they were coming back to the hotel for some girl time, Emma and I made our way down the hill toward our limo. Richard and Adam were waiting outside the car, smoking.

"When did this start back up?" I whispered to Emma.

"Do you really have to ask?"

I waited outside the car with Richard while everyone got in. I had the feeling he wanted to say something, and sure enough he did.

"Look, I'm sorry about the whole smoking thing." He ran his fingers through his hair.

"It's okay. I understand."

"I'll quit. I swear."

"Richard . . ." I said with a smile, raising my hand and resting it on the side of his face. "It's okay."

He calmed instantly and sighed, leaning into my hand and nodding.

We made it back to the hotel quickly, and Emma and I explained to the guys that we just needed some girl time alone in my room. They seemed hesitant at first, but we finally came to an understanding—and I promised to leave the adjacent door unlocked to Richard's room so they could come and check on us at any time.

I quickly showered and changed as the others did the same, and by the time I got out of the bathroom all the girls were sitting on my bed, arms full with every little bottle of alcohol they had in the mini fridge. We sat in silence for a minute, looking at the large pile of booze that sat before us— and feeling brave, I picked up the small bottle of Jack and opened it.

"To Ruth," I said, lifting the bottle in front of me.

Sara picked one and opened it, clinking it against mine. "To Nina."

Kandace laughed and opened a bottle, too. "To Linda. Lord knows that crazy bitch is looking down at us, pissed off that she's missing out."

Emma picked a bottle, opened it, and sighed. "To making it."

Anna lifted her bottle of water and rubbed her belly with her other hand. "To our sisters," she said, looking over at me.

We all smiled and pounded down our drinks. It had been a while since any of us had drunk alcohol, so we all kinda had a hard time with choking down that first round. By the seventh, we were all starting to unwind. Well, all but Anna.

"Can I just say something?" Kandace slurred, sipping her drink. "Was it me or did that bastard have the worst breath ever?"

"Kandace," Anna groaned. "We swore not to talk about him."

"I know, but come on . . . you have to admit—"

"Yes," Sara and I said at the same time.

"Can I ask something?" Emma whispered. We all nodded for her to continue. "I know I didn't have it as bad as the rest of you, but am I the only one that has to sleep with the lights on?"

"Hell no." Kandace laughed. "I sleep with everything on."

Emma looked over at me and I nodded in agreement. "Don't worry, you're not the only one," I said.

"I don't want to be here," Sara said, looking at her empty drink with teary eyes.

"Neither do I."

"Where the hell do you want to go?" Anna asked.

"I want to have a drink with *all* my sisters," I whispered, clutching the small bottle in my hand.

"You are," Emma said.

"No, we're not." Kandace looked at me and nodded.

"No," Anna said quickly. "No way. It's locked up and my fat ass is not jumping any gates."

"Come on, Anna," I pleaded. "They had their time to say goodbye, and now it's our time."

"Lee, I—"

"They put them in the ground, Anna," I yelled. I got off the bed and pulled my shoes on.

"Lee, where are you going?" Sara asked.

"I'll go alone. I don't care, but I don't want to be here," I said in a rush, grabbing a sweater and pulling it on.

"Well, I'm in," Kandace said, taking the rest of the booze and slipping it into the pockets of her robe. She turned around and looked at Sara and Emma. "You coming?"

"Why not?" Sara replied. "I've got nothing better to do."

I looked over at Emma who gave me a small smile.

"Are you sure, Emma?" I asked.

"Positive."

I didn't know what Emma said to Richard and Adam, but less than an hour later we were standing outside the gates to the cemetery.

"Again I say, how are we going to get my fat ass over this?" Anna groaned.

Before any of us could answer, Kandace started to climb up the gate.

"You are fucking crazy." Sara laughed.

"And so am I." I sighed, following Kandace up the gate.

Soon Kandace, myself, Emma, and Sara were on the other side of the gate waiting on Anna to join us.

"Come on, Anna. It's really not that bad," Emma promised.

"You guys better catch me if I fall," Anna yelled, starting to climb up the gate. We all cheered once her feet touched the ground on the other side. We started to walk away when Richard called out for me.

"Be careful," he whispered, reaching out and touching my face as soon as I returned to the gate.

"I will." I smiled, leaning into his touch. "Thank you, you know, for doing this."

He smiled and nodded. "Go do what you gotta do."

It was easy to find the grave site. I guess the workers were going to wait until the morning to remove all the flower arrangements and photos. We stood there silently, each of us in our own world. I was more than confident that the others were thinking about what they went through down in that hole, but I wasn't. I couldn't. My thoughts were only on the three faces that seemed to be staring back at me from their pictures.

I had never even known Nina, but I clearly felt some type of burden seeing her face. It was as if I failed her, too. Not by not saving her, but by not giving her the justice she deserved. My eyes scanned over Linda's picture quickly, unable to find the strength to look into her eyes. Linda was a perfect example that he could have killed any one of us at any moment. I fought back the tears when I turned to Ruth's picture, so innocent and sweet. I could still hear the sound of her neck being snapped as if it were happening right next to me.

I took a step forward and gazed down at Ruth's grave. "I'm sorry. It should have been me."

"What?" Anna yelled.

"No, honey." Emma sniffled, coming over to my side and trying to wrap her arm around me, but I shrugged her off. "Lee, without you none of us would have made it."

"She's right, Lee," Kandace whispered.

I turned around, feeling annoyed at their lack of understanding and yelled, which caused the girls to move back a step. "You didn't see it happen. You didn't see the look on her face when he came from behind and wrapped his hands around her neck."

I felt bad when I saw the looks on their faces, but what was worse was the feeling of the tears that were threatening to spill over. I was tired of crying; it seemed that was all I had been doing. I turned around and glared at the pictures of Nina, Linda, and Ruth.

"I swore to myself that I would avenge their murders. That he would suffer till his last breath for what he did to you all, and I failed." I staggered a little bit, letting the last word fall from my lips in a whisper.

"What do you mean 'what he did to us'?" Kandace demanded. "Lee, he did it to you, too. He deserves to suffer just as much for what he did to you. It's not your—"

"Yes, it is," I yelled. "I was ready to go. I made my peace, and was ready to take him down with me." I don't know why I started to walk away, but I had to. Standing there reminded me of my failure. "I want to know why," I screamed. "Why did it have to be them? I was stronger than them. I was more of a threat. I made sure of it, and yet he took them. He ripped them out of this world like they were *nothing*, and I want to know *why*!"

I couldn't hold it back anymore; I let the tears flow freely. "I had his life in the palm of my hands, twice, and yet I'm still that weak little girl stuck in the basement." I fell to my knees and gripped my hair tight in my hands. "I had him, down there. I could have bashed his face in, or snapped his neck, but I was *weak*!" My voice caused the girls to jump. "And then when I had the chance again, I blew it." I was sobbing now. I wrapped my arms around myself, feeling like my body was going to explode at any moment. "It should have been me." I whimpered, leaning forward and resting my forehead on the cold ground.

I heard footsteps coming toward me and felt the grass shift. Too tired to protest, I didn't flinch when I felt a hand glide over my hair. "We all feel that way, Lee," Sara replied. One by one, I felt each girl come around me and rest their hands on my back.

"I just don't know what to do," I cried into the ground.

"We do what we need to do to make sure he can't do this again," Anna answered.

"And we speak for the ones who didn't make it," Emma added.

"And we make sure that when he gets to jail, he shares a cell with the biggest, baddest inmate in that fucking place," Kandace said, causing us all to giggle.

We all sat together, crying for what felt like hours, before anyone spoke.

"Do you think any of us will be normal again?" Sara asked.

"We have to try," I answered, sitting up and looking around at the girls. "We owe it to the others not to let him destroy us, but I can't do it alone. I don't know how to."

"Then we'll figure it out together." Anna smiled, stroking my hair.

We all nodded in silence at her words, but I wasn't sure if I believed what she was saying, or even what I had said. It felt impossible at the moment to think I would ever be normal again.

"We should start heading back." Emma sighed. "The guys are probably freaking out."

"Then let's get this over with." Kandace smiled, reaching into her pocket and pulling out a small bottle of alcohol for each of us. We turned and faced the graves of our fallen sisters.

"To Ruth." I choked back a sob as I downed my drink.

"To Linda," Sara said firmly as she and Emma drank theirs.

"To Nina." Kandace smiled, taking the shot quickly and letting out a sigh.

We all looked at Anna as she opened her shot and dumped it into the grass. "To all of us."

We stood up and said our last goodbyes to our sisters. I felt different looking at their pictures. I couldn't explain it, and I didn't even want to try. Whatever I was feeling was better than what I had felt before, and I was okay with that.

"I'm still going to live up to my promise," I whispered, unsure if I was saying it to myself or to them.

I looked down when I felt a hand grasp mine, and smiled when I saw that it was Emma's.

"And I'm going to help," she said.

"Me, too," Anna said, coming up and wrapping her arm around my other side. One by one the girls came forward and declared their promise to help me. We were making our peace, our promise, and standing there together as one, I had never felt stronger.

Chapter17

Six Months Later
—Richard

I sat in my car, shaking, wishing that this damn cigarette would calm my fucking nerves. I had thought I could handle this. I'd felt ready.

When Noah called to say that David Reed had been released from the hospital and was going to be interviewed by Agent Chase, and that he could get us into the viewing room, I knew I had to go. I had to know. I needed to hear from him why Reed wanted her. Why my girl? Why *my* Lee?

With a knock on my window, I looked over and saw Noah standing outside my door. I quickly got out and waited for him to put out his cigarette.

"You ready for this?" he asked.

"I don't know," I answered honestly. "But I need to know why, so I guess I'm as ready as I'll ever be."

Noah and I were ushered into a dark, empty room once we made it inside. There was a large glass window, which allowed us to see into the interview room where Reed was being led. Noah reassured me that David wouldn't be able to see us, but I wasn't stupid. Even though he didn't know who was on the other side of the glass, it still didn't stop him from looking at it and smiling after he was secured to the table.

I felt a moment of pride when I saw the damage that Lee had caused to his face. Both his upper and lower lip looked to have been sliced open; they were marred by a long, ragged scar that hadn't quite healed right. He also had a bandage that went from just below his chin to his upper chest and disappeared below his jumpsuit.

"Why have they waited so long to do this interview?"

"That bullet did a lot of damage to him, on top of the injuries he received from Lee," Noah replied. "Chase wanted to make sure that Reed was off the pain meds, and coherent, before doing this. They want him at full strength so his lawyer can't claim needing a continuance to heal. He was also under the influence of some heavy narcotics, and we wanted to make sure he was considered stable before questioning him."

Agent Chase entered the interrogation room and threw a file across the table toward Reed. Photos came spilling out in front of him, and I inched closer to the glass to get a better look. It was a file that held photos of the girls, alive and dead. Some of them were even crime scene photos taken of the girls after they were found in the forest.

Reed gingerly held out his finger and placed it on top of one of the pictures, turning it, and dragging it toward himself. He looked down at it and smiled. "She had promise. Too bad someone had to go and mess with her head. She'd still be alive."

The mere sound of his voice disgusted me, but I couldn't help but smile at the obvious lisp he had courtesy of the scar Lee gave him.

"You want to elaborate on that? Tell me what happened to Ruth-Ann Summers," Agent Chase said calmly.

"No." Reed smiled, pushing the photo away.

Agent Chase calmly took the head shots of the girls—the ones they showed on the news and in newspapers—and lined them up next to each other. "You had great taste in women, David," Chase said. "Each one very beautiful, and talented in some way."

"They are, aren't they?" Reed said with pride.

"Out of curiosity, who was your favorite?" Chase asked.

"All of them," Reed answered quickly.

With a slight tilt of his head, Chase chuckled. "Really? All of them?"

"They each had special qualities." He grinned, placing his cuffed hands in his lap. "They all fed a desire I needed fulfilled."

Chase only nodded and slid a photograph out of the lineup toward Reed. "What need did Kandace fill?"

"My excitement," he answered, his lips causing him to trip over his words.

"Excitement? Huh," Chase murmured, scratching his head. "I wouldn't have guessed that. You see, I've had the pleasure of meeting Kandace, and I must say I wouldn't expect someone so mouthy to—"

"That's what makes her exciting, though." Reed smiled. "To unlock that door and not know what she was going to do or say." He ran his tongue over his bottom lip and I couldn't help but shiver. "Very exciting," he purred.

"And Ruth?" Chase asked, pushing her photo toward Reed again. "Was she exciting?"

"No." Reed sighed, shaking his head. "Ruth was innocence. Innocence in its purest form." He raised his hands from over his head and placed them on top of Ruth's picture. "To touch something so soft, so precious. Having her mouth around me was like slipping into a warm bath."

I nearly vomited. He was talking about these girls like they were lovers. I wanted to break through the glass and rip his fucking head off.

"So you enjoyed having sex with them? It wasn't about pain?" Chase asked. I couldn't understand how Chase seemed so calm, so collected. It was baffling.

Reed sighed again and pulled two photos toward him, lightly stroking them. "I wanted to give them pleasure. I wanted them to feel my love for them. They were exquisite." He lined up the four photos, and as I looked closer, I saw that they were the pictures of Kandace, Linda, Ruth, and Nina.

"So why did you murder them?" Chase asked, pointing to the three at the end.

"To save them," Reed said softly.

"Save them from what?"

Reed just smiled and shrugged.

"And you only chose these girls? Why not the others?"

"I was going to prepare Kandace that night, but I was rudely interrupted," he growled.

Chase pulled back all the photos, but then lined four others in their stead. They were photos of Anna, Sara, Emma, and Lee. "So tell me, if these women weren't for saving, what was their purpose?"

Reed looked down at the photos with a menacing face. He quickly reached over to Emma's picture, lifted it, and flipped it to face Chase. "She was nothing to me. She was Tom's." He tossed the photo on the floor and shook his head. "I would have never looked twice at that girl."

"I was given the impression you fancied her?" Chase asked.

"Sure, I would have fucked her, but she was too weak," Reed answered in a very matter-of-fact manner.

"And the others? What was their part in all this?" Chase pushed the three leftover pictures forward a little more.

Reed took another picture and flipped it over, holding it up. It was Anna. "She was about pain. She was my muse for getting out my frustrations." I could feel my anger grow by the second. He looked so smug as he continued talking. "She'd make a great submissive; never talking back, always following orders. Well, until the end."

He threw the photo on the floor and it landed next to Emma's.

"And this one . . ." He chuckled, reaching for Sara's picture next. "She was about suffering, and man, did I make her suffer. She was like my guinea pig for ideas I wanted to try with the others."

I heard a growl behind me and looked over to see Noah start to pace. We were thinking the same thing—Reed was saving Lee for last.

Chase seemed to pause for a bit and then reached for Lee's picture, but Reed beat him to it by tossing Sara's picture on the floor and snatching Lee's. He stared at it for a long time and then smiled.

"I love this girl," he whispered.

"Really?" Chase leaned back in his chair.

"Lilly is the rarest type of woman," he purred, rubbing his thumb over the picture.

Noah came up to the glass so fast that it rattled a little. He was breathing hard, and looked like he was about to scream.

"You love the woman who got you caught, who permanently disfigured you, and is the reason you'll live the rest of your life in jail?"

Reed just shrugged.

"What was Lee to you?" Chase asked.

"Her strength." He smiled. "I wanted to destroy it the second I saw it in her."

"Then why did you only rape her once?" Chase pried.

"She wasn't for that. She was a spontaneous choice, compared to these others. I didn't know how strong and willful she was until I had her. Once I saw it, I wanted to destroy that. The more she fought back, the harder I hit." He shook his head and chuckled. "Man, she could take a hit. A lot better than any of the other girls." Reed looked up at the glass and for a moment I could have sworn he could see Noah and me. "But when I was inside her, thrusting into that beautifully bruised body, it was heaven."

It was my turn to growl at that point.

"Does it bother you?" Reed yelled, still looking at the mirror, at us.

"Knowing I know your sister better than you? Knowing that I will have a piece of her that you will never touch?" An eerie smile swept across his face. "And although she'll never admit it, a small part of her, deep down, loved every second of it."

"You son of a bitch," Noah screamed, flying out of the room, and reaching for the door that went to the interrogation room. I ran after him and grasped his arm as he tried to open the door. Another officer nearby helped me pull him away as Agent Chase exited the room.

"I'll fucking kill him. I swear to God I will," Noah screamed.

"Get him out of here," Chase yelled, and the officer took Noah away.

I stood there in silence as Agent Chase talked to another agent. He seemed very deep in conversation, so I took the opportunity to slip into Reed's room unnoticed.

He sneered as I shut the door behind me. "Don't you think you're a little too old to be playing cops and robbers, Richard?"

"It's good to know I don't have to go through mundane introductions and pleasantries with you," I replied, locking the door.

"So, what? Come to fight for your beloved Lilly's honor? I'd thought we could be friends. Swap stories." He laughed.

"No." I smiled, shaking my head and walking toward him, trying to keep my nerves in check. "I'm not here for Lee." I could see the slight worry in his eyes as I stopped in front of him. "But I'm not here to be your friend either, only to promise you something."

"Promise me what?"

I leaned forward, but just far enough that he couldn't reach out for me. "You will get what's coming to you."

Before he could say anything in response, I pulled back my fist and hit him as hard as I could in the face. His head flew back like a rag doll, and it took every ounce of self-control I had not to hit the bastard again. Lee needed me, and I'd be useless to her locked up in a cell next to this piece of shit, although that *was* an intriguing idea. Pulling myself together, I straightened up, walked out of the room, and all but ran out of the police station.

———

I arrived back at the apartment just in time to see Adam carrying the last of Emma's things out. Once she had been released from the hospital and the police had allowed the girls back into their homes, Emma had packed up most of her things and moved into Adam's room. At first it bothered me, but I knew Emma needed that security, and so I pushed my brotherly emotions aside and moved in with Lee. I wanted . . . no, needed to be closer to her anyway.

"You ready for tampons, pink crap, and leaving the toilet seat down?" I asked, taking one of the boxes out of his hands and walking with it toward his truck.

"Are you?"

I just laughed. We might have joked about it, but this was what we'd both wanted for a while.

"Is Emma saying goodbye to Lee?"

"No," he answered, looking over at the apartment and then back at me. "Lee had a rough day. I think Emma leaving upset her, but she won't admit it. She knows Emma needs this, so she took something to help her relax and went to sleep."

"Thanks, bro. I appreciate you looking out for both of them."

Emma had tears in her eyes when she came outside and gave me a hug, making me promise for the hundredth time that I'd call her if I needed her. I knew she felt like a bad friend for leaving Lee, but before they drove away, Adam and I both reminded her that she needed to feel safe, too.

When I walked back into the apartment, I stopped in the hallway outside Lee's bedroom door. Light shone from beneath it, and it killed me to know that she still needed the lights on to be able to sleep. Even with the lights on, she sometimes woke up screaming in the middle of the night. I would rush into her room, hold her hand, and whisper my love for her until she fell back asleep. But if I even tried to get in the bed to hold her, she would all but jump out.

I started thinking how Lee had changed, little things that made me nervous, things that I didn't understand until I'd asked Noah about them. He told me most female rape victims felt better sleeping with their shoes on, changing the locks to the house, adding bars to windows, carrying mace, and sticking to strict schedules. It was their way of trying to feel safe and in control.

Sometimes I couldn't help but feel that I might not be enough for her. That even with me being here with her every night, she still might not feel safe. I just wish I knew what I could do. My instincts told me to go in her room, wrap her in my arms, and comfort her. But it would be like putting a bandage over a gaping wound. Lee needed time to heal, and all I could do was hope that one day she'd let me in again so I could help.

—————ᴧ∧ᴧ—————

—*Lillian*

"So did Richard go with you to see Anna and the baby at the hospital?"

"No."

"Because you asked him not to?"

"Yes."

"Why?"

My therapist, Joanna, had been recommended by the state because she specialized in helping women who had experienced traumatic situations. Everyone said that it would help, and the other girls were seeing her, too, but I hated every minute of our sessions.

How could this person know what to say if she hadn't gone through anything remotely similar herself?

When I said as much to my mom, she'd tried feeding me the idea of group counseling. But I shot her suggestion down real quick. Last thing I needed was a bunch of strangers looking at me like I was some kind of freak.

"Fine, we'll get back to that," she said, looking down at her notebook and writing something when I didn't answer. I hated that fucking notebook. "So tell me, Lee, how is your relationship with Richard going?"

She'd asked me this question at the end of almost every session, and I'd never answer it. But for some reason the words came spilling out on this day.

"I'm thinking of breaking up with him," I said.

She looked a little shocked by my answer, and set down her pen and paper. "Did he do something wrong?" she asked, sitting back in her chair.

"No."

"Is he being pushy or forceful in any way?"

"No, not at all." *He's been an angel.*

"Has he said anyth—"

"He deserves someone who isn't damaged," I said. "He deserves to be touched, and kissed, and . . . he just deserves more."

I loved Richard with all my heart. He had always been there for me. He let me cry when I needed to cry, gave me space, and loved me when I allowed it, but he needed more. More than I could give.

It hurt me to see his face look so deflated when I'd pull away from him, or turn my head away from a kiss. I wanted to kiss him, to hold him and never let go, but I couldn't. *He* had kissed my lips. *He* had touched my skin. No matter how hard I'd scrubbed my body, *he* still lingered there. He had burned himself onto me. And it was a scar that only I could see.

"Do you not deserve love?" Joanna asked. "If Richard is not expecting these forms of affection, then why break away and end a good thing?"

Because I'm damaged goods. "I don't know," I whispered, wiping a small tear away. "I just don't feel I'm ready for what he needs, but I don't want to lose him."

Joanna looked up at the clock and clicked her tongue. "I want you to do something for me, Lee. I want you to talk to Richard about these feelings." I looked at her like she was crazy. "I'm serious," she said, with a little force in her tone. "I bet you haven't even started preparing yourself for the trial next week, because you're too focused on why you're not good enough for Richard."

I glanced over at the calendar that sat on Joanna's desk. Was it April already? The trial was scheduled to start the first week of May, and with that asshole damned near back to perfect health, the state was eager to get the ball rolling.

"You've been losing days again, haven't you?"

"I'll talk to him," I replied, ignoring the question. I didn't want to talk about my constant sleeping or spacing out. Weeks would go by and I wouldn't know. If it wasn't for Richard, I wouldn't even know it was Tuesday. Therapy day.

"If you love Richard as much as you feel you do then, in my opinion, talk it out. If you two need me, or even if you need to talk to me about it, you know you can call me at any time."

Her words stuck with me as I left the building, and I found myself not only thinking of Richard, but the other girls as well.

They all seemed to be getting better in some small way. Sara and Kandace dove right back into school, needing the distraction and normalcy again. Anna and I chose to take some time off. Anna had the better reason, being pregnant and then having the baby, but . . . I just didn't want to think about school. I wasn't ready yet. I appreciated that nobody pushed me about my decision. As if it would have mattered.

As always, Richard was outside waiting for me. Always with a smile on his face and a cup of coffee in his hand. Before, when I had come home from a session with Joanna, I'd go right to bed and sleep until the next day.

Richard thought if he got some coffee in my system it would keep me awake for a little while, hoping to get me to talk. Of course, we never talked about what he wanted to talk about, but I liked hearing about his classes, or about what Luke had done that day. I even caught myself laughing a few times when Richard talked about Luke going off on Adam for being too loud with Emma in the other room.

"No brother should ever hear that shit," Luke would complain.

We sat in silence this time. It made me feel a little nervous. Richard was never silent after my sessions. I guess it was a good thing. It allowed me to think about what Joanna and I had talked about. *Did I really want to let Richard go? Could I imagine a life without him?* I knew the answers to these questions already. It was a no-brainer. I just didn't know if I needed him more than he needed me.

Once we got home, I was relieved that no one was there. My mother had left shortly before Emma did, having stayed in Boulder until all her family leave ran out. She still came up at least twice a month, but I was happy that today it was only going to be the two of us.

Instead of walking to my room, like I always did, I went over to the couch and sat down.

"We need to talk."

I looked up at Richard and saw a mix of fear and excitement in his eyes.

"Okay," he said, coming over and sitting next to me.

"I'm sorry that I've been so distant," I whispered, restraining myself from saying *undeserving*.

"You don't need to apologize for that, Lee."

I took a deep breath and stared straight ahead. "I think we need to—"

"Don't," he said. "Don't say it."

I sighed and rested my head in my hands. "You don't understand."

"You're right, I don't," Richard said, obviously upset. "I can't for the life of me understand why you feel you don't deserve to be loved." He shifted in front of me and sat on the table facing me. "Why do you have this idea that we can't get through this together?"

"I don't know," I whispered. "I'm not the same girl you once knew. Not anymore."

"Bullshit!"

"I'm broken. I'll never feel right . . . think right."

"Bullshit."

"You deserve better, all right?" I cried. "Fine, you want to know how I feel? You think you're ready? I live in a constant state of fear." I kept my eyes on him the whole time, willing my tears to maintain their distance. "I fall asleep every night, knowing I'm going to be dreaming of that man's breath on my face, hearing the screams of the girls as he raped them, and I don't know when it's going to stop . . . if it will ever stop. You deserve a girl who . . . you just deserve more, Richard. I love you, but I'm not enough for you."

I kept my eyes on him as I watched him take in my words. His face was a kaleidoscope of emotions. I was about to get up when he stood and lifted me off the couch. He pushed me into my room and stood me in front of my mirror.

"Look at yourself," he whispered. I tried to pull away from his grasp, but he wouldn't let me go. He moved himself behind me and rested his forehead on the back of my head. "Please, Lee, just look."

I looked up slowly and stared at my reflection. One word came to mind whenever I looked at myself. Broken.

Richard stood up straight and looked over my head to gaze at my reflection. "I'm going to say this one time, and then I never want to hear the words 'you deserve more' come out of your mouth again." He closed his eyes and took a deep breath. "Do you have any idea how much I love you?" he whispered.

I could already feel the tears start to prickle behind my eyes.

"Do you have any idea how much I want this?" he asked, wrapping his arms around me and pulling me to his chest. "I wouldn't care if you were bald with scars running down your face, and had the most disgusting form of athlete's foot I'd ever seen. I'd still want you."

I rolled my eyes, trying to hide the tear that fell down my cheek.

"No," he said, turning me around so I was facing him. He fell to his knees and hugged me around my waist, resting his cheek against my stomach. "Please, believe me. Believe me when I say I love you more than anything."

I bit my lip to hold back the sob that threatened to explode out of my body. I lowered myself onto my knees and cupped his face in my hands. He looked so scared, so worried. I ran my thumb over his cheek trying to comfort him in some small way.

"I know," I whispered. "Please, Richard, don't think for one second that I don't love you, too."

"Then what do I have to do?" He trembled, resting his hands over mine. "What do I have to do to show you how much I need you? How much I have to have you in my life?"

I couldn't hold back my sobs any longer. I crumbled as his words kept pouring out.

"I want to marry you, Lillian. I want to fall asleep next to you while resting my hand over your growing belly. I want to come home after a long day of work, and see you smile as our children come running toward me. I want to argue with you, cry with you, grow old with you, and I know you might not want these things right now, if ever, but I need you to know that I do. I will be here until you tell me to go."

I couldn't believe these feelings, these words that seemed to wrap around me like a warm breeze. A feeling I didn't think would ever exist for me again.

I wrapped my arms around him, and held him as tight as I could. "Y-yes," I whispered.

I felt him exhale against my hair. "Yes?"

I nodded in haste. "Yes."

He pulled back and cupped my face, gazing into my eyes. "Yes?"

I couldn't help but laugh. He looked as if I was speaking in a foreign language. I took his hand off my cheek and lifted it to my lips, pressing a firm kiss to it.

"I want all that, too, Richard," I said, rubbing my cheek against his hand. "I want to feel your children grow inside me, wake up every morning and see you next to me, and be with you as we grow old and ugly." We both laughed through our tears and I moved his hair away from his eyes. "I know it won't be easy, and that we'll butt heads the whole way, but there is no one I want to be with. So yes, Richard, my answer is yes."

Richard's chest started to shake as a smile spread across his face. A loud laugh erupted from his lips.

"Yes!" he yelled, standing to his feet. "She said yes!" He bent down and wrapped his arms around me and lifted me up, twirling me around. "Oh my God, Lee . . ."

He placed me back on the floor, but still held onto me. He looked into my eyes and lowered his forehead to mine. We stood there for what felt like hours, just holding each other. We were looking into each other's eyes as if we were having some bizarre staring contest. For the first time in months, I had the need to show my love for him. To prove to him how much I needed him, just as much as he needed me.

His eyes widened a little as I moved my lips toward him. His demeanor completely changed in a second. He went from happy to ecstatic with a simple swipe of his tongue over his bottom lip. Taking a shallow breath, I closed my eyes and pressed my lips to his. I had missed that warmth, that tingle I would get whenever our lips touched. His hand came up into my hair and massaged my scalp. I sighed against his lips and smiled.

"I love you," I whispered.

"Always," he whispered back, capturing my lips again.

—◦◦◦—

Chapter 18

—Richard

I jerked in my seat as Judge Cooper slammed her gavel against the wood. It was day three of the trial, and each day had been more unbearable than the last.

"Mister Williams, please try to control your client." Judge Cooper sighed, tossing her gavel across her desk. "I do not appreciate these outbursts in my courtroom."

"Yes, Your Honor." The defense attorney appointed by the state—an asshole named Williams—leaned over and whispered in David Reed's ear. He was a monster, a soulless beast walking the earth, and I wished I could choke the life out of him with my bare hands. Both him and his shady-ass lawyer.

Anna Lin was on the stand, being questioned by the prosecution. She was having a hard time keeping it together, which was understandable considering that the man who had raped, tortured and humiliated her for over five months was sitting just across the room from her with a smug grin on his face. I wished she didn't have to go through this, nor any of the girls for that matter, but I had faith in them that they would pull through.

"Anna, please continue. Tell the court how you obtained some of your scars," Ms. Howard, the prosecutor, asked.

"He enjoyed burning me with a lighter when he came into my room,"

Anna answered.

"Objection," Williams called out. "How could she possibly know what my client enjoyed or did not enjoy?"

I wanted to jump over the rail and castrate the fucker.

"Sustained," the judge said.

Ms. Howard just smiled, nodded, and faced Anna again. "Anna, what gave you the impression that the defendant enjoyed torturing you with a lighter?"

"Objection!" Williams said again.

"I'm only asking for my witness' opinion, Your Honor," Ms. Howard countered quickly.

The judge nodded. "Overruled."

Ms. Howard motioned for Anna to continue.

"He would laugh when I begged him to stop. He even did it sometimes when he was . . ." Anna couldn't finish. She started crying right there on the stand.

I had to force my eyes to not wonder toward Reed. I was afraid that if I even looked at him I wouldn't be able to stop myself. The feelings running through my body didn't seem natural. I couldn't have described them even if someone were to ask. Hearing what Anna had gone through, and knowing it was what all of them—even my Lee—had gone through, filled me with a hatred that bordered on insanity.

"Your Honor, can we please give the witness a few minutes to collect herself?" Ms. Howard asked.

Judge Cooper looked at her watch and nodded. "We'll take a short break. Be back in fifteen." And with a smack of the gavel, we all stood up as the judge left the room and Anna rushed out of the witness stand.

Luke, Adam, and I, along with my parents, Sadie, Noah, and the rest of the girls' families, slowly began making our way out of the courtroom behind Anna when a soft whistling stopped us in our tracks.

It was the jackass, Reed.

Anna stopped and spun around, shaking and looking like she was about to collapse, but I quickly reached out and caught her. Tears fell from her eyes when she gazed up at me.

"That son of a bitch." I glared over Anna's shoulder to where Reed sat.

He continued whistling, and I recognized it as the tune of the song Lee had told me Reed always played when they were underground.

"What it is?" Luke asked.

"It's the song," I answered. "That fucking song he always played when he left the girls alone in that place."

Behind us, a woman's voice hitched and a man cursed, but all I could see was red. It was as if I was a bull and Reed was the red flag.

"Get me out of here," Anna whimpered, clinging on to my shirt.

I continued to glare at Reed and he smiled like he didn't have a care in the world.

Suddenly, Adam was standing in front of me, blocking my view. "Go. Get her out of here, Richard."

As soon as we made it out of the courtroom, I handed Anna to someone—her parents, I assumed—and rushed to the bathroom. I paced a few times in front of the mirror before making my way to the last stall and slamming the door shut behind me. I wanted to hit something, hit it so hard it would release all the anger I felt in my body. But instead of pounding my fist against the wall, I pressed my back against it and slid down until my ass hit the ground with a thud.

I sat on the cold tile floor, tapping the back of my head against the wall as I tried to control my breathing and prayed for my body to calm down. Lee needed me strong. I hadn't seen her since we arrived, which was hours ago. She'd been taken to a secluded room somewhere until it was her turn on the witness stand. When it came, the last thing I wanted was for her, or that asshole, to see that he'd gotten to me.

After a while, I heard the bathroom door open, and the clicking of shoes on linoleum.

"Richard?" Luke called.

"Yeah."

"It's Lee's turn on the stand."

What? I looked down at my watch, and sure enough almost two hours had passed. I stood and opened the stall door. My brother waited in silence as I went over to the sink and splashed some cold water on my face. I looked up and glared at my reflection.

I glanced over at Luke through the mirror before reaching over and pulling out a few paper towels to wipe the water off my face.

"How did Anna do? Did she make it though the rest of her testimony all right?"

"She did good, real good, but we better hurry."

Nodding, I took one last look at myself before walking past Luke and out the door.

—⁓—

"Miss Locke, could you please tell the jury what a typical encounter with the defendant was like during your time in captivity?" Ms. Howard asked.

Lee had appeared calm when she was sworn in, but I knew it was a mask she was wearing to fool everyone. As she'd sat down, I'd caught a glimpse of her right hand, which looked like she had scratched it raw. It was a nervous habit she developed since she got home from the hospital.

I wasn't surprised that the prosecution wasted no time getting right into the meat and potatoes of Lee's story. They had already spent a whole day going over questions to prepare her for this, but all that preparation didn't seem to make it easier on her.

"He would come into my room and beat me, sometimes touch me," she answered with a steady voice.

"Touch you?" Ms. Howard asked as I tried to push down the acid that was creeping up my throat. "Over the clothes? Under the clothes?"

"Both. Over and under."

"What were some of the things he would say?"

Lee looked at her brother and mother, who were sitting next to me. "He would call me names, threaten my life, and even threaten my family's lives."

Ms. Howard nodded and walked over to her table, picked up a notepad, and then faced Lee again. "I want you to try to remember October eleventh, ten days after your kidnapping. The day Ruth-Ann Summers was murdered."

Lee started tapping her heel against the floor.

"How did that day begin?" Ms. Howard asked.

Lee closed her eyes and took a deep breath. "Anna woke me up," she said slowly. She opened her eyes and looked straight at me. "She tapped on my wall and kept calling out my name until I woke up."

"What happened next?" Ms. Howard asked.

Still looking at me, she let a tear roll down her face. "I heard *him* in Ruth's room, moaning. Ruth was crying out in pain, over and over. I knew by then that he didn't like being called names, so I decided to pick a fight with him to get him away from Ruth."

Wait, what?

"And by *him*, you mean the defendant, David Reed," Ms. Howard said.

"That's correct."

Why didn't Lee ever tell me this?

"Why did you do that?" she asked.

Lee glanced back at Ms. Howard and ran the back of her hand under her nose, wiping away the wet residue. "She was just a child. I had to get him away from her."

To say I was proud of Lee would have been an understatement, but it still broke my heart. And, even though she was going through this whole process to put David Reed behind bars for life, it was almost as if he was getting one last shot at torturing her since she had to relive the experience all over again.

"What happened next?"

"I called him names and taunted him until he left her room and came into mine. He left her door open when he came over . . ." Lee trailed off and a look of pain flashed across her face.

Helplessness washed over me. I was afraid of what she would say next. She'd told me once, vaguely, how Ruth had died, but it was clear I didn't know everything.

"Miss Locke . . ." Lee's eyes seemed to glaze over. "Miss Locke . . ." Her face became pale and she slouched forward a little in her chair. "Miss Locke . . ."

When her hands began to shake I was ready to run over there and take her home. She didn't need this. None of them did.

"Miss Locke," Judge Cooper said, tapping her gavel against her desk.

"Sorry," Lee whispered, wiping away her tears once again.

"Do you need a minute?" the judge asked.

She shook her head and looked over at Ms. Howard, who smiled and nodded before giving Lee a small wink. "What happened when the defendant came into your room?"

"He beat me, strangled me, threatened to kill me." Her voice sounded robotic and dull.

"How did you survive?"

"I fought back, clawing and hitting him as best as I could."

My eyes burned and my throat closed up as I imagined it, but Lee continued without emotion.

"He got mad at me for not giving in, then went across the hall and hit Ruth so hard that it knocked her out. Then he came back into my room and kicked me in the face, also causing me to black out."

I took a deep breath and lowered my head to my hands, clenching my eyes shut. A hand rested on my shoulder and I sat back up to see it was Luke. The pain in his eyes told me he was just as hurt and upset as I was.

"And then what happened?" Ms. Howard asked. I held my breath.

"I woke up and saw that my door was still open. I could see into Ruth's room."

"So Ruth's door was also left open?" Ms. Howard turned toward the jury.

"Yes."

"Could you see Ruth?"

"Yes. She was still out cold. The other girls and I called out to her until she finally woke up. That's when she realized she wasn't chained to the wall anymore."

"How did Ruth become unchained?" Ms. Howard asked.

"I'm not sure." Lee blinked slowly, dazed for a second. "She just stood up and the chain was gone."

"Did you ask Ruth to come into your room?"

Lee shook her head. "No, I told her to stay where she was, but she didn't listen. As soon as she stepped into the hallway, he came out and snapped her neck."

"The defendant?" Ms. Howard asked, motioning toward Reed.

No, it was fucking Santa Claus, you box of rocks.

"Yes," Lee whispered.

"Miss Locke, could you please tell the jury how you managed to escape from your cell?" Ms. Howard smiled, walking over to the jury, and leaned against the wooden rail.

Lee took a deep breath and raised her eyes to mine. I forced a smile and nodded, praying that she could see not only how much I loved her, but how proud I was of her. I regained my composure while she told the jury about the holes they dug in the ground between their cells, and how they'd exchanged Anna's bobby pins. Lee explained how she used them to unscrew the bolts on the wall, which had given her the scars that still covered the insides of her hands. Ms. Howard had her raise them, palms up, so the jury could see them. Lee described how she waited for Reed once she'd gotten free, and how she'd provoked him to open her door.

"When you hit the defendant with the metal plate, did you think he was dead?" Ms. Howard asked.

"Yes."

"And when you stepped out of your room, what did you see?"

She closed her eyes and took a shallow breath. "Darkness. Everything was dark. There was a soft light overhead, but it took a while for my eyes to adjust. I could tell I was in a hallway, but I couldn't see anything else around me."

"Where was the defendant at the time?"

"He was on the floor. When I hit him, he fell, and it caused his body to fall against the door across the hall from mine, causing it to open."

"And that's where you found Miss Haines?" Ms. Howard asked, and Lee nodded. "Was she alone?"

"No," she said, clenching her eyes tighter. "Tom was in there with her."

"That would be Thomas Reed, the defendant's brother. Correct?"

"Yes."

"What did he say to you?"

"He told me to go, to take the others and leave—all except for Emma. I had to leave Emma behind."

Lee started to shake, and I began hoping that Ms. Howard would call a recess or something, but she just kept pushing.

"And what was your response to that?"

"I said no. I could never leave any of them behind."

"Is that when Tom attacked you?"

"Objection," the defense attorney yelled. "Leading."

I wasn't sure Lee heard anything after that. When she opened her eyes, she turned toward Mr. Williams, and unfortunately toward Reed. He was staring at her and smiling, as if he was having the time of his life. His eyes were fixed on her and all I could think about was beating the shit out of him. He had no right to look at her ever again. I forced my attention back to Lee, who nearly jumped out of her seat when Ms. Howard touched her arm.

"Do you need me to repeat the question, Miss Locke?" she asked, giving Lee a reassuring smile.

Lee nodded and ran her hand through her hair. "Please."

"What happened after you told Thomas you wouldn't leave without Ms. Haines?"

"He came after me. He . . ." She paused and took a deep breath. "He tried to kill me."

"How did you get away?"

"I gouged his eyes and then, when he rolled off of me, I hit him with the plaque." Lee bit her lip and rubbed her fingers over her forehead. "He didn't get up after that."

Ms. Howard read Lee's police statement to the jury, recounting the incident and how Lee found each of the girls in their rooms, before asking her next question.

"After you realized that you couldn't free any of the girls, and had moved the defendant's body into your room, what did you do?"

"I used the keys that Tom had to open the metal door at the end of the hallway. Then I walked up the stairs until I came to an open hatch."

"What did you see then?"

"When I climbed out, I found myself in some kind of broken-down cabin. The roof was falling in, and there were pieces of broken wood and trash everywhere. I looked for a phone, but I didn't find anything except a locked box and a stereo."

"Was there a door? Were you locked in?" Ms. Howard asked.

Lee shook her head. "No, there was no door. I was able to walk right out."

I wanted her to look over at me at that moment. To look into my eyes so that she could see the happiness in mine at the memory of how she'd walked out into the moonlight and found me waiting for her, but she didn't. She kept her head down while she finished her story, up until the point she was shot—after that she couldn't remember anything.

"Thank you, Miss Locke," Ms. Howard said. "No further questions."

Lee sat in silence, keeping her eyes to the floor, as the judge asked the defense if they had any questions for the witness. And, of course, the asshole did. My heart sped when Williams stood from his chair and made his way toward Lee.

―⁓―

"What a fucking asshole," Emma yelled from the kitchen later that night.

"Which one?" Luke chuckled, taking a swig of his beer. "They were all assholes, in my opinion."

"The defense attorney," Emma said. "How does he even sleep at night?"

Williams was a first-rate asshole, and had spent several minutes badgering Lee after the prosecution had finished with her. Fortunately, Judge Cooper put a stop to it and court was adjourned for the day.

After we'd left the courthouse, Emma, Luke, and Adam had followed Lee and I back to our apartment. As soon as we'd walked through the door, Lee went straight to her room and fell asleep. I was so worried about her. I wanted so badly to hold her in my arms, caress her hair and tell her how much I loved her, but I knew she needed her space. We hadn't told anyone about the engagement yet, knowing she wanted to wait until after the trial, but it still didn't stop me from reminding her every chance I could. It was always in simple ways—rubbing my thumb over her ring finger, telling her how I couldn't wait to spend the rest of my life with her, and when I was lucky, sharing another heated kiss.

"All I'm saying is that the guy better get the death penalty," Emma hissed, walking back into the room and pulling me out of my thoughts.

She passed out another round of beers and perched herself on Adam's lap. I couldn't help but feel a slight twinge of jealousy seeing how Emma and Adam were with each other. I missed the way Lee would fall into my lap every chance she got. She used to say it was the best seat in the house.

"Colorado may have the death penalty, but they've only executed one person on death row since 1977," Adam said.

Yeah, we'd looked that shit up. Both of us had wanted to know how that fucker would die if he did get it. After researching the shit out of 'Capital punishment in Colorado' on the Internet, what we found astonished us.

"So what are you saying? You don't think he'll get it?" Luke asked.

"How much do you know about this shit, Luke?" I asked. "Have you ever looked it up?"

"Oh yeah, every day, man." He smirked.

I ran my hand through my hair and sighed. "No, he's not going to die, not by the state anyway."

"How do you know?" Emma asked. "I mean, look what he—"

"Because all he has to do is plead guilty before the trial is over, and the state will just turn around and give him life in prison, but that's if he pleads guilty," I said. "Look it up."

"Damn." Luke sighed. "And if he did get it, how would he die?"

"Lethal injection."

"That's it? I thought they would at least have the chair here."

"He deserves worse," Emma whispered.

I looked up at her and our eyes met. I nodded in agreement, then looked over at the clock and noticed that three hours had gone by and still no Lee.

"Hey, do you think you guys could scatter?" I asked. "Give me a few hours alone with Lee?"

"Sure." Emma nodded, standing and taking Adam's hand in hers before gesturing to Luke to get up.

After the door closed behind them, I moved around the room, picking up the empty beer bottles and random crap, and threw them away in the kitchen trash. Once everything was back to how it should be, I walked quietly into Lee's dark room.

I sat in a chair and watched her sleep. She looked so peaceful, so . . . I couldn't explain it. For a second it was as if the last six months hadn't happened. It was as if I was looking at the old Lee. *Old Lee*. I shook my head in annoyance. I couldn't help but remember the last time Lee and I had been intimate. I had memorized every touch, every kiss, every soft word that escaped her lips. I prayed for the day that I would be able to make her feel that way again—to make her feel beautiful, cherished, and safe.

I felt the faint vibration of my phone in my pocket, and slipped out of Lee's room before answering it. It was Noah.

"I'm outside," he said simply.

I tossed my phone on the kitchen counter as I made my way to the front door.

"Were you able to get the cabin?" I asked, letting him in.

"Yeah, I got it," he answered in a mild tone. I walked over to the patio door and opened it to have a smoke. "It's pretty secluded and you two shouldn't have a problem with privacy. Just make sure you put chains on the tires before heading up." Noah paused and looked down for a moment before looking back up. "Are you sure this is a good idea?"

"Noah, she needs this. You always said she loved going up there, that she loved the peace of the forest."

"I know," Noah said. "I just think it might be too soon."

"Please just trust me on this, okay?"

I decided the minute the judge said *guilty*, I was going to take Lee away for a while; she needed space and comfort. Noah said a buddy of his on the force had a cabin up in the mountains that we could use for as long as we needed it. I couldn't wait until the morning to tell Lee, but Noah was still a little reluctant.

"Fine, but the second something feels off, you bring her back. If she says she doesn't want to go, you accept it. Understand?"

Just then a soft whimper echoed throughout the apartment, followed by the stumbling of feet, and the bathroom door shutting. I winced when I heard Lee coughing over the toilet.

"I understand, but I think it's the best idea I've ever had."

—⁓—

Chapter 19

—Richard

"Mr. Reed, what was life like for you and your brother growing up?" Williams asked.

For some reason Reed looked over at me, and I took the time to lift Lee's hand to my mouth and kiss it, smiling as I watched the fire burn in his eyes. The fucker could kiss my ass.

"Tough," he replied. "We moved around a lot, and didn't have a real father figure in our lives."

Boo-fucking-hoo.

"And who raised you and your brother?"

"Our mother."

Williams walked over to the defendant's table and grabbed a folder. He opened it up and started reading. "Your mother is Wendi Reed, alias Wendi Tusk, alias Wendi Moore, alias Wendi Davis, alias Wendi Firn, alias Wendi Nichols. All these aliases were from marriages she had before you turned eighteen, correct?"

"Yes," Reed said firmly. "That's correct."

"That must have been hard, growing up watching your mother bounce from man to man like that."

Reed just shrugged. "They each had a purpose for my mom, nothing more. None of them lasted more than a few years."

"What do you mean by purpose?" Williams asked.

"One man paid for her boob job, another paid for her liposuction. Face lifts, new cars, houses. The last one you named was old enough to be her grandfather, and when he died he left her everything. So like I said, they all had a purpose."

I didn't get what the point to all of this was. So his mom was an old whore? Big deal.

"Were any of these men abusive to you or your brother?"

"No," Reed replied. "None of them had anything to do with us."

"That must have hurt," Williams said, looking at the jury with sympathy in his eyes. I wanted to gag.

"That's how my mother wanted it."

"What do you mean by that?"

Reed leaned back in his chair and sighed. "My mother didn't want us to grow attached to people who wouldn't be in our lives for long, and vice versa. They were hers, and only hers. My brother and I were to just wait until it was time to leave."

"And during the times when your mother wasn't married, what was that like for you and your brother?"

"It was rough. My mom would be out trying to find a new john, so it was just my brother and I."

"So at a young age, you were forced to be an adult, and raise your brother," Williams said, looking over at the jury.

"That's right," Reed said proudly.

"David, do you think that due to your lack of a mother and father figure in you and your brother's lives, this must have been why your brother stalked and kidnapped these young ladies?"

If I wasn't sitting down, I would have fallen over. *This* was the defense attorney's strategy? They were going to try and pin it all on Tom? Fucking pathetic.

"I believe so, yes."

"Objection," the prosecuting attorney yelled. "How can the defendant possibly assume why Thomas Reed kidnapped any of these victims, unless the defendant was the one who told him to do it?"

"Unfortunately, due to Miss Locke's actions, we'll never know exactly why," Williams replied. "But I think we can all agree that his brother, the defendant, would be the best person to ask. No one here, including his mother, knew the deceased better than my client."

I noticed that Reed glanced toward the back of the room, and I looked over my shoulder to see an older woman wearing large dark glasses. She was fair skinned with bright blond hair, and was wearing a dark blue suit. She almost looked asleep with the way she just stared ahead, body stiff like a statue, but I noticed how her fists flexed every few seconds. Then it hit me, this was Reed's mother. A part of me wished she'd take her glasses off so I could get a better look at her, and the other part wanted to walk over to her and ask if she was proud of the pieces of shit she'd made.

"I'll allow it," the judge said with a nod.

"I have no further questions," Williams said, smiling at Ms. Howard.

Before the judge could tell Ms. Howard it was her turn, she was in front of Reed.

"So you're telling us that your brother, on his own, was the one who stalked and kidnapped all the victims? Is that correct?"

"Yes," Reed answered.

"And he alone took them to your place of work, up at the Black Rose Mines, and chained them underground at an abandoned cabin."

"Yes."

Ms. Howard nodded and walked over to the jury. "David, did your brother hold a gun to your head and force you to rape and beat these women?"

Reed paused and then sighed.

"No."

"Did Thomas say he was going to kill you, or threaten you in any way if you didn't participate?"

"No."

"So why do it?" Ms. Howard asked. "Why put yourself out there to get caught and put in jail, for your brother's crime? Why not, I don't know, call the police?"

There was a long pause, and it took me a moment to realize that it wasn't because Reed was trying to think of another bullshit answer. It was because he was staring at us. I watched as his eyes wandered from each of the girls before settling on Lee. I looked over at Lee and watched in shock as she mouthed 'pussy' to him, and then turned her head away and looked out the window.

I looked back over at Reed when I heard a growl echo throughout the courtroom. It was insane how he went from calm and collected to angry and ready to strike in a matter of seconds. And then I realized it was because of Lee. She knew exactly how to get under his skin.

"Do I need to repeat the question, Mr. Reed?" Ms. Howard asked, taking a few steps closer to the witness stand.

"No, I heard you the first time, you dumb bitch!" Reed yelled, causing all the girls and the rest of the courtroom to gasp. "I did it because I wanted to, and there was no one there to stop me. Look how long I had them." He leaned all the way forward and pointed right at Lee. "They were all mine until that whore came along and fucked everything up. They're still mine, and they know it."

The clicking of Ms. Howard's shoes was the only sound we heard as she walked the rest of the way to Reed, leaning forward and getting in his face.

"Unless you want me to add perjury to the long list of charges on your indictment, I recommend you recant your story right now and tell us the truth."

Reed looked at Ms. Howard and then Lee with disdain. Williams stayed quiet as Reed turned back to Ms. Howard and opened his mouth.

—∿∿—

Several Weeks Later

"Ladies and gentlemen of the jury, have you reached a verdict?" the judge asked.

"We have, Your Honor."

"What say you?"

The bailiff walked over to the foreman, took a piece of paper from his hand, and delivered it to the judge. The judge looked at it, her face not giving away any hint of the verdict. She folded the paper and gave it back to the bailiff, who returned it to the jury foreman. Judge Cooper nodded for them to continue, and the foreman started reading. I felt Lee's hand tighten around mine as the verdicts were read.

"We, the jury, find the defendant on the first count of first degree murder of Nina Rosado, guilty. On the second count of first degree murder of Ruth-Ann Summers, guilty. On the third count of first degree murder of Linda Baker, guilty. On the first count of kidnapping and unlawful restraint of Anna Linn, guilty. On the second count of kidnapping and unlawful restraint of Kandace Veccio, guilty. On the third count of kidnapping and unlawful restraint of Sara Turner, guilty. On the fourth count of kidnapping and unlawful restraint of Lillian Locke, guilty. On the fifth count of kidnapping and unlawful restraint of Emma Haines, guilty."

I wrapped my arm around Lee when I felt her body start to shake. I looked up at the judge and watched her nod at the jury before asking, "So say you all?"

They kept their eyes on the judge as they each nodded.

For some reason, I looked over at Adam at that moment, and he was looking straight at Reed. I followed his line of sight and almost jumped out of my seat. Reed was staring right at us. No, not at us, at Lee. I lifted my hand and covered Lee's face, knowing he enjoyed seeing tears pour from her eyes. As soon as his view was impeded, his gaze bounced up at mine and he smiled.

"Thank you, ladies and gentlemen of the jury, you have done your job well," Judge Cooper said.

"Your Honor," Williams said, standing up. "I believe at the beginning of this trial my client wished to be sentenced as soon as the verdict was read."

I looked over at Adam again, but he was still staring at Reed.

"Very well," the judge answered.

My heart sank, knowing what was going to happen, and I was hoping that there could have been a way to protect Lee and the girls from it. I looked over at Reed and growled. Of course he had a smile on his face. This was his last act to cause them pain. He knew what he was doing.

"I can't even begin to imagine the pain and suffering you girls went through." The judge sighed. "And I hope that after today you all can rest easy knowing Mr. Reed will *never* be able to hurt you *ever* again."

Lee's head popped up at that moment.

Judge Cooper looked over at Reed. "David Reed, in the twenty years that I have been a judge, I have never seen anything like this. In my opinion, your brother got off easy. With that being said, Mr. Reed, I am sentencing you to death by lethal injection. You will be placed at the Sterling Correctional Facility where you will wait on death row until a date is announced. May God have mercy on your soul. Court is adjourned."

As soon as the judge's gavel hit her desk, Lee stood up, tripping over my legs. I helped her right herself, only to have her rip her hand from mine as she fled the courtroom. Everyone else watched Reed being taken away by the bailiff and two corrections officers. He looked like he didn't have a care in the world, or like he was off on some great vacation. I wanted nothing more than to jump over the barrier and beat him to death, but I couldn't. Lee needed me and she was my number one priority.

When I finally caught up to Lee outside the courtroom, we were bombarded by cameras and reporters asking us if we were satisfied with the judge sentencing the last Black Rose Killer to the death penalty.

The Black Rose Killers. That's what they were calling David and Thomas Reed. I found it disgusting, but it didn't shock me. The entire country had taken to this story like it was some crappy reality television show. Every major network was there, trying to talk to anyone who could give them an exclusive.

When we pushed through the sea of reporters and made it to our car, Lee let out a scream.

"I'm supposed to be the one that did it! Their way is too humane, too kind. I want it to be me! It was my job, my promise, and all he's going to do is slip into darkness and never wake up. He needs to suffer, feel some ounce of pain. He needs to experience for one night what he put us through."

I pulled her to me as she started sobbing against my chest. She just kept saying over and over that she was supposed to do it. That she should have killed him when she had the chance.

"I love you, baby," I whispered, kissing her hair. "I'm sorry that this is bothering you so much."

Once she'd calmed down, I drove us back to the apartment. Every once in awhile I would lift our joined hands and lift them to my mouth, kissing her knuckles lightly, wishing I could do more to comfort her. She never said a word the whole time, going straight to her room once we got home. I knew she wanted to be alone, but it took everything in me not to go in and comfort her.

It seemed as if everyone went to bed after we got home. Luke went home, saying he was going to enjoy some silence since Adam and Emma were staying over. Emma was asleep in her old room, so Adam and I were the only ones left up. It was two in the morning, and I was more than annoyed that the few rounds of beer that we had shared had done nothing for my rattled nerves.

"Lee is gonna kick your ass for smoking in the house," Adam said, laughing.

"I think this is one of the few times she's not gonna care." I chuckled, blowing out my smoke.

Just then Lee's voice cried out, but it wasn't the normal type of hysteria that escaped her at night. It was frantic, even bone chilling.

I leaped up and ran into her room. She was lying in her bed, thrashing around, screaming out my name. In the almost seven months that she had been back, she had not once cried out for me. I went to her bedside and picked her up, settled her on my lap, and held her against my chest.

"I'm here, baby. I'm here," I whispered, rocking her back and forth. I heard the door creak behind me and turned my neck in time to see Adam close the door to give us some privacy.

"He just kept kicking and kicking," she said, crying against my chest. "But it wasn't in that room, it was here. He was in *my* room, Richard. In my room!"

I lifted her chin up so she had to look at me. "Never," I said. "He will never touch you again, Lee. I promise you . . . I swear to it."

I felt my body shake with anger. Anger because I had never seen such fear in her eyes before, a fear that that son of a bitch had put in her. I knew I was the only one who saw this side of her. I didn't know why she had to put up so many walls around other people, but I was relieved that she broke them down for me.

"I just wish I could forget him, for one night. Just forget it all," she whispered.

"Me, too, baby." I nodded. "I would do anything to take your pain away . . . even for one night."

Lee's eyes trailed down for a second, and I sat there waiting. I didn't know what to do, what to say, but she seemed deep in thought so I stayed silent. Suddenly I felt her warm palm rest against my chest. I followed her line of sight and saw that she was focused on her hand pressed against my chest. With love and determination in her eyes, she slid it up, and cupped around my neck. I closed my eyes when I felt her nails scrape against my scalp.

I don't think this is a good idea.

Lee sat up and then straddled my hips, lifting her other hand, and resting it against my cheek.

Not a good idea, Richard. Not in the slightest.

So delicately that I almost didn't feel it, her lips ghosted over mine.

"Lee, I . . ." I whispered, still keeping my eyes shut.

"Please, Richard," she whispered. "If I die tomorrow, if some freakish accident should happen, I don't want his hands to have been the last hands that touched me."

Her statement jarred me, and I opened my eyes and was met with two of the most beautiful eyes I had ever seen. I could see the pain in them, the agony that still haunted her, and for that I couldn't go any further. I could understand the reasoning—hell, I wouldn't want that man to be the last thing to touch me either—but I couldn't let her relieve the pain this way. Not the way she wanted me to.

I cupped her face in my hands and pressed my lips firmly against hers. "Come with me," I whispered, standing up. I took her hand in mine and led her into the bathroom.

Once inside, I turned on the water and made sure the temperature was just right. When I turned around, I couldn't help but smile at the look of utter confusion on Lee's face. Wanting to ease her bewilderment, I slowly walked over to her and kissed her forehead.

"I love you, Lee," I whispered. "More than you'll ever know."

"I love you, too."

Slowly I reached behind her and unzipped the back of her dress. I let my fingertips glide up her arms and to her shoulders, where I hooked my thumbs under the straps of her dress so it pooled at her feet when it fell. I let my lips feather over her forehead again while I reached behind her a second time and unhooked her bra.

"Turn around," I murmured, and smiled as she did so with no hesitation.

Leaving my hands on Lee's hips, I trailed warm kisses down her spine until I was on my knees. I let my hands move up and rest right below her breast, as I swiped my tongue over the small scars that were scattered over her back. Even the scar from her bullet wound, which made me shudder every time I saw it, and remained bright red and puckered over her upper right shoulder months later. I had wanted to cry out in anger the first time I saw the marks on her porcelain skin, and seeing them now didn't make me feel much different, but this was about Lee. This was about making her feel good again, even for just one night.

A moan escaped from her lips and I felt myself grow hard. I moved my hands up and, very carefully, pulled at the bottom of her bra, allowing it to fall on the floor with her dress. I rested my forehead against her lower back as I let my hands continue up, and brushed my fingertips against her soft breasts. I couldn't help but smile when she sucked in a tight breath, and then exhaled it with a low moan.

"Are you okay?" I whispered, hoping I wasn't moving too fast for her.

"Yes," she breathed out, as I let my thumbs rub against her pebbled peaks.

I opened my eyes and looked at the dainty white pair of panties that my beloved was wearing. Feeling somewhat eager, I trailed my fingers down her sides to the elastic on her underwear. Inch by inch I carefully lowered them, allowing my tongue to glide over the exposed skin as it unveiled itself before me. I had to curb my inner hunger. I was becoming harder by the minute, and seeing Lee like this was not helping me tame my inner male asshole who wanted to throw her down and take her. It had been over half a year since I'd been intimate with Lee, and my body wanted to dive in and claim her back, but I wouldn't. She wasn't ready for that—and to be honest, neither was I.

I stood up and removed the band that was holding Lee's hair up in a loose ponytail. I swept her hair over to one shoulder and kissed the exposed skin. I closed my eyes and straightened up. "Get in before it gets cold. I'll be there with you soon."

I didn't touch her as she walked around me and got into the shower. I stood there for a second, calming myself down and reminding myself to take it slow with her.

She didn't need to be told again how strong she was, because deep down she knew that already. She didn't need to be told that she was a survivor because she made it out alive. She needed to be reminded that she was beautiful, that she was mine, and that I was hers. I could tell by looking in her eyes that she knew it, but didn't feel it. I had to show her, to have her feel it, to have her remember how good we felt together.

I stripped off my clothes and walked into the shower. Her back was to me, her hair already soaked, and instantly I felt myself start to weaken. I couldn't help but let my eyes dance over the water that was cascading down her firm body. It was a beautiful thing. I could write songs about that ass alone. I reached forward and let my arm wrap around her waist, as I moved my other arm to wrap around her chest, pulling her tight against me.

"You are so beautiful, baby," I moaned, feeling myself rub against her smooth ass. "I can't wait to make you come again."

"Please," she panted, rubbing herself against me.

Biting back a moan, I let my hand trail down her stomach and toward her heated core, while I let the other cup over Lee's perky breast.

"Oh God, yes," she whispered as my finger swept between her wet lips and over her soft clit.

"Does it feel good?" I smiled, rubbing my fingers over it again, this time applying a little more pressure.

"Oh Richard, please," she said as I let my fingers slide lower, circling over her dripping opening.

"Tell me," I whispered into her ear, causing her to shudder. "Tell me what you want."

"I need to feel you. Richard, please, I need to feel you in me," she said, as she bucked her hips against my hand.

Running the tip of my tongue along her ear, I let two of my fingers dip into her warm center. I let my palm grind against her swollen clit as I rubbed myself against her again.

We stood there, panting, moaning, and whispering words of love, as I moved my fingers faster and harder inside her. I felt her knees starting to grow weak as her walls began to tighten around my fingers.

"That's it, baby," I said. "Let go."

"Richard," she whispered, bucking her hips even faster.

"I love you, Lillian. My love, my forever, and soon . . . my wife."

And with those words, she gripped one hand into my hair and the other over my unrelenting fingers, and let go.

—Lillian

I lay in bed with Richard, naked, watching the sun rise. The warm colors cascaded over his tanned skin as they peeked between the soft blue curtains that we should have closed last night.

After our shower, I fell asleep quickly, and for the first night in months, stayed that way for the rest of the night. No nightmares of David and Thomas, no waking up crying, just wonderful, blissful dreams full of Richard and me—finishing school, getting married, starting a family, and living the rest of our lives in peace and quiet.

Looking over at the bedside clock, and seeing that it was still early, I was surprised when I felt Richard stir next to me.

"Good morning," he said, letting out a soft yawn and kissing my hair.

He pulled me against his bare chest and squeezed me tight.

"Good morning."

"I love waking up like this. We need to make this part of our everyday routine," he said with a smile. "Now all we need is the caffeine IV bag and I'll be in heaven."

I sat up and draped myself over his body, leaning down and rubbing my nose against his. "Still with the IV bag?" I whispered.

Richard wrapped his arms around me and pulled me flush against his body. "I don't know, you seem to be waking me up just fine. Maybe I don't need it."

I couldn't help but laugh. "You are such a romantic."

He gave me a soft kiss before pulling back. "How are you feeling?"

"I'm good, but I also feel bad that I couldn't . . . you know, do more last night."

Richard moved me to the side so he could sit up. "Why would you feel that way? I didn't give you the impression that I wanted to—"

"No, not at all," I said. "I just . . . I don't know."

"Hey," he whispered, pulling me beside him and holding my hand. "There is no rush. It's not a race to try and get back to where we were. We'll get there in our own time. Okay?"

I smiled and nodded, words failing me because all I wanted to do was wrap my arms around him and cry. Richard just felt too good to be true sometimes, and I found myself wanting to pinch my skin to make sure I still wasn't dreaming. And he was mine. He wanted to marry me. There was nothing else I wanted more than to be his wife.

"So what are your plans for today?" he asked, reaching over to the side table and grabbing his glasses so he could put them on.

I sighed and leaned back in bed, wrapping the blankets tight around me.

"This," I said, faking a yawn. "I plan on being the biggest lazy-body in the world."

I watched as Richard got up and put his pajama pants on.

"Well, I'm sorry to tell you, but that's not going to fit into my plans."

"Oh, really?" I said, closing my eyes and pretending to fall asleep. "And what are your plans?"

I felt the bed move and opened my eyes to see Richard hovering over me, a boyish smile spread across his face.

"You and I are driving to a cabin in the mountains for some much needed R and R."

"Are you serious?"

"As a heart attack," he said, kissing my forehead and getting off the bed. "So get up because I'm making breakfast, and as soon as you are packed, we are heading out."

I watched as Richard walked out of our room and into the kitchen where I heard him humming and pulling out the pans from the cabinet. Enjoying my good mood, and excited about the trip Richard had planned for us, I decided to call Anna while he made breakfast. I didn't know why, but I wanted to hear her voice. Her phone didn't ring, but went straight to voice mail. I almost didn't want to leave a message, but found myself talking before I could stop myself.

"Hey, Anna. It's Lee. I just wanted to let you know that Richard and I are going to be out of town, and cell reception is crap where we're going." I smiled and paused. "For the first time in a while, I'm starting to think that everything is going to be okay. That we are all going to be okay." I stopped for a second when I saw Richard standing in the door frame, a goofy grin stretched across his face. "I love you, Anna. Talk to you soon and kiss that baby for me."

I hung up and tossed my cell on the bed.

"You are, you know?" Richard said.

"I am what?"

He walked forward and wrapped his arms around me.

"You're going to be okay. All of you are."

I leaned my forehead against his chest and took a deep breath, his scent filling my lungs and bathing me in love and comfort.

"Promise?" I whispered.

He kissed the top of my head and tightened his hold around me.

"I promise."

—*ɯɯ*—

Acknowledgement

I would like to thank my friends and family for all their support in helping me achieve this unbelievable accomplishment. Thank you to my wonderful team of remarkable ladies who have helped me finish this book: Tyggy, Adri, Heather, Wendy, Jenny, Christine D., and everyone at The Writer's Coffee Shop Publishing House.

About the Author

Kris Thompson is a veteran of the US Navy and single mother of three. When she's not knitting scarves, chasing her children around or baking, you'll find her enjoying a good book or writing down notes for her own upcoming stories. Writing has been a passion for Kris for many years, and seeing those stories printed on paper is a dream come true.

CPSIA information can be obtained at www.ICGtesting.com
Printed in the USA
LVOW05s1110141114

413720LV00013B/136/P